NAUGHTY LITTLE GIFT

A TEMPTATION COURT NOVEL

ANGEL PAYNE

NAUGHTY LITTLE GIFT

A TEMPTATION COURT NOVEL

ANGEL PAYNE

WATERHOUSE PRESS

"The declaration of love marks the transition from chance to destiny, and that's why it is so perilous..."

— Alain Badiou

CHAPTER ONE

MISHELLA

"Dear, sweet Creator. That man's ass needs its own web page."

"Right?"

"Maybe it already has one. Have we tried looking it up? What would that search string even be?"

"*Cassian Court's Glorious Glutes?*"

"Sounds about right."

I scowl at the exchange between my best friend and my princess of a boss. Debate adding a huff, though that might make them giggle harder. As it is, Vylet lifts her head, lets the wind blow her black waves as if she is shooting a scene for a movie, and slowly bats the thick lashes framing her huge lavender eyes.

"Is there an issue, Mistress Santelle?"

Her purposeful drawl on the *s*'s turns her query into a tease—though before I can properly purse my lips, she is answered by a long, snorting laugh. I add a groan to my own response, stabbed at the sound's source. Brooke Cimarron, Princess of the Island of Arcadia, might have the loyalty and love of thousands across our land, but her royal in-laws are not in that legion—and outbursts like that are no help to her cause at all.

The groan might be forgotten, but the sigh is not. Even after three months in her employ, my work is still clearly cut out for me. In my princess's own words, I am to do everything in my power to "whip the royal decorum into shape." Some days, the task is easy. Some, like today...are entries in the *Sweet Creator Help Me* journal.

I have one of those. Literally. Though on the outside, as I observe right now, the book simply says *Action Items*.

Despite the lists taunting me from the pages of said journal, there are many more checks in Brooke's "plus" column than not. Brooke has a good heart, a willing spirit, and a loyalty to Arcadia rivaling that of many native-born to the island. If I can only work out a way to keep Vy from enabling the woman's snarky American side...

Not likely anytime soon.

Most certainly not during this week.

Cassian Court's arrival in Arcadia has sealed that certainty solidly enough.

Cassian Court. Just rolling my mind over the man's name jolts me with such intense heat, I wonder if the Earth has rolled too quickly on its axis, shifting my chair into the sun instead of beneath the table on the Palais Arcadia lawn. That only forms the start of how he has upended my world in just two days.

Two. Days.

Cassian Court.

I cannot help myself. The syllables are synonymous with so many other expressions. *Engineering genius. Corporate wizard. Billionaire icon. Consultant to kings.* Yes, that includes the leader of our land, Evrest Cimarron, who has invited his friend for a "modernization think tank" with Arcadia's leaders. Yanking a kingdom forward by two hundred years in two days is no small feat.

Two. Days.

World. Upended.

Not to mention my thoughts. And my bloodstream. And the very wiring of my nervous system...

"Mishella?"

Vylet's playful prompt is perfectly timed. "Hmm?" I am grateful to leave behind a memory that has been taunting, of the man in his formal wear from the party King Evrest threw for him last night. Out of respect for Arcadian tradition, he wore a doublet-style jacket with his tailored Tom Ford pants, everything flawlessly fitted to his tapered torso and long legs. The black garment had featured one modern touch: a moss-green zipper instead of buttons, drawing out the same shade in his eyes. Matching zippers had adorned his hip boots, making him look very much "at home" in the ballroom's courtly crowd...

"You truly have no comment?" The edges of Vy's lips curl up. Little wench. She knows I would sooner watch a storm come in over the sea than have to look at the body part they've referred to on Cassian Court's incredible form.

Incredible.

And magnificent.

And breath-stealing.

And, in just two days, has made me painfully aware of how small my island home truly is. The man and his magnetic pull have actually made me yearn for a land as big as his, though the expanse of America still does not seem big enough for all these new feelings he inspires—sensations that sweep in again as I gaze upon him training at swords with Jagger Foxx on the palais lawn.

Dizzy.

Giddy.

Hot.

Needy.

No.

I cannot. I will not.

Instead, I compress my lips harder. Swing another censuring look at my friend. "I was being courteous, in deference to Her Highness."

"Oh, here we go again," Brooke mutters.

Vylet hides a laugh behind her elegant fingers. "But Mishella wants to practice her protocol, *Your Highness.*"

Brooke glowers. "Am I going to kick *your* ass about this now too?"

"Not in that pretty tea frock, missy."

"Oh, even *in* this rag, ho-bag."

"Who you calling ho...*ho?*"

"Say it twice because I own that, baby." Brooke swirls and then stabs an index finger. "Especially after last night's marathon under that man of mine."

"Ohhh!" Vy roller coasters the syllable with knowing emphasis. "And I thought you were just walking funny from the platform pumps."

"See how I did that? Gotta have a cover, girl."

They snicker harder than before. I fume deeper than before. Attempt a prim glance down at my lap but only get two seconds of the reprieve. A fresh punch of testosterone hits the air, swinging all our stares back up.

By everything that is holy.

The masculine energy is well supported. Even a hundred feet away, the two men are like gladiators of old, shirtless bodies lunging, gleaming muscles coiling. Jagger Foxx, the Arcadian court's lieutenant of military operations, does not give his American guest an inch of visitor's courtesy—a handicap Court would take as an insult anyway.

The result is...

Glorious.

Slanted forward, his body forty-five degrees from the lawn, Cassian Court is a breath-stealing study of sinew, strength, might, and motivation. His thighs, clearly etched beneath his white fencing pants, wield the force of a stallion. His torso, the color of a lion in the sun, coils with equal power.

Their blades clash. Metallic collisions *zing* the air. Jagger stumbles back. Again. Grunts hard—though not as deeply as the man besting him. Just like that, Cassian Court turns into an even more exhilarating sight. His beauty is meant for the glory of physical triumph.

All the heavens help me, I cannot stop staring. Or wondering. What would it feel like...to be held by those massive arms? What would it be like to lie beneath that beautiful body? To spread my legs, allowing his hardness against my welcoming softness...my tight readiness...

My throat turns into the Sahara. I swallow, coughing softly as the moisture clashes with the dryness.

"Holy hell," Brooke murmurs.

"Which has to be where I'm going, after what I just imagined about that man."

Vy's confession welcomes new knives of confusion. Logically, I should be reassured. My reaction to Court is not unique or special. But another part, new and foreign, fights the urge to think otherwise. To scratch her eyes out for sliding into my territory.

As Brooke would eloquently put it: *what the hell?*

Men are a complicated subject in my life—contradicted

by their very simplicity. They are like clothing or cars or office tools: needed but not coveted, functional but not desirable. Yes, some exist in higher-end form, but I do not think of them longer than the time it takes to interact with them. I do not dare. Father and Mother will eventually use me as a pawn to gain what they want from one. It might be the twenty-first century, but politics are politics—and world-changing decisions are still made by the heads between men's legs, not the ones on their shoulders. I have to be grateful for reaching my twenty-second year without having to bother with it yet.

But I will.

And lingering lustings for Cassian Court will not make it any easier.

"*Pffft*." Brooke flings the comeback at Vy while reaching across the glass table for her sun tea. At least Brooke *looks* like a princess today, the pale-blue tea dress coaxing matching sparkles in her eyes, the daisy-yellow sweater matching her platform pumps. Shockingly, she has listened to my suggestion of wearing a pearl necklace and earrings with the ensemble. "We're mated, not entombed." But looks can be deceiving. Her saucy smirk proves it. "Besides, neither of us is the treasure who's caught Mr. Court's eye—and likely some other body parts."

Mortification. While I debate whether to let it curl me into a ball or send me under the table, Vy erupts in laughter. "True that, sistah!"

At least that helps with the decision. No shrinking now. I fire off a new glare. "Have you two gotten into the nectar?" I am half-serious. Nipping at the Arcadian fruit wine, followed by sitting in today's ruthless sun, would be a reasonable explanation for their giddy moods.

"Right." Brooke leads on the response, laughing wryly. "We could only wish."

Vy echoes the snicker. "Word to the princess."

They collide fists in a punching motion, followed by fanning and wiggling their fingers, prompting my fresh fume. It is a joke. I *know* that. I also admit these are confusing times for everyone in Arcadia. Our country is emerging from two hundred years of self-imposed separation from the world into a reality where nearly everything has changed. The adjustment is unsettling at times, even to Brooke, who was born American but has lived here for the last seven years.

Now, she wears the gold band on her left hand declaring her legally married to Prince Samsyn—a detail Vy enjoys forgetting whenever they get together. That turns me into the reminder police.

"Do not forget your place, Vylet Hester. Brooke is your *princess.*"

I delete the part about Brooke having been the kingdom's actual queen for a week—seven days she never wants to remember again, though they have brought one joyous result. At the time, she needed a *secran* as soon as possible, so I entered her employ—and found a purpose I never thought possible for my life. For the first time, I am no longer Fortin Santelle's pretty trinket of a daughter or even a faceless Arcadian court clerk, filing and typing my days away. Brooke depends on me. Confides in me. Relies on me for input on everything from appropriate clothing choices to modern political issues from a native Arcadian's point of view. It is a serious responsibility, and I never take it lightly—despite the fact that she sometimes does.

"Okay, listen up, missy." The woman herself sets her drink

down so hard, some of the tea sloshes out. "If you don't loosen that caboose and relax a little, I'll have to personally hunt up some nectar for *you*."

And sometimes, she *completely* forgets. Like now.

"Yes! Do it!"

"No. *No*."

My response overlaps with Vy's, doubling our volumes into an outburst across the lawn—enough to freeze the men in mid-clash. But only one of them adds a concerned glance, giving his opponent a crucial second of advantage. It is the only second Jagger needs. With a shout, he plunges. With a grunt, Cassian goes down.

With a gasp, I lurch to my feet.

Just as swiftly, I sit back down. Too late. The damage is wrought. My chair has certainly sprung flames, since they waste no time climbing to my face. Vy and Brooke give me no mercy, either. They actually clap as I sit there, drowning in embarrassment, and continue the racket so long, the men obviously assume the praise is for them. Well, *Jagger* does. As soon as he helps Cassian up, turning both their bodies into gleaming masterpieces of sun-drenched muscle, he sweeps a gloating bow.

Brooke and Vy laugh even harder.

Shockingly, my lips twinge. Their joy *might* be a little contagious...and the day *is* perfect, with the breeze carrying salty moisture bites off the ocean, along with jasmine and orange from the trees. A little laughter cannot be such a crime. Perhaps it is...therapeutic. I am not a prude—I grew up in the back halls of the Arcadian Court, after all—but talking about lust and experiencing it firsthand are two separate things. *Entirely*. I have spent the last two days as skittish as a toddler at her first swimming lesson. Everyone has to get in and paddle sometime, though taking oneself too seriously can only be dangerous.

A perfect reassurance...

Until I swing my sights up, to watch Cassian Court approaching across the grass.

Striding like a king.

Rippling like an Olympian.

Staring like a hitman.

At me.

Laughter, meet shredder. Throat, get back to the desert. Composure...

Composure has gone rogue—doing whatever it bloody well wants. My mind is frozen, but my sex is incinerated, cranking the intensity with every smooth, sure step with which the man dominates the lawn. By the time he and Jagger stop beneath the table's wide umbrella, my hands are a rigid ball in my lap and my breaths are rapid pumps against my flower-print dress—which is suddenly, completely, too tight. Oh sweet Creator, how he makes my breasts throb...and ache.

And *tingle?*

"Oh...*my.*" I keep it to a whisper for my ears alone. *Miracle.* My hand flies up to assuage my racing heartbeat. I easily disguise the action by fiddling with the polished piece of Minos Reef coral suspended around my neck. Usually, the purple trinket lends me focus and strength. Not now. Not even close. Not with Cassian Court continuing with his unflinching stare at me...his unyielding *examination.* I cannot help but note every nuance of his gaze. Even in this blazing heat, it is the color of cool forests. I am drawn to thoughts of waterfalls and lagoons in those glades...and him swimming in them, drenched and naked.

By the powers...

When his features crunch, horror sets in. I've blurted it aloud. Can he read the thought that has prompted it too? Does he know the lewd turn of my mind—and his importance in it?

Oh crap oh crap oh crap...

And now, I am as guilty as Vy of borrowing the vulgar Americanism. But that is where I have descended. Where *he* has made me fall.

"Miss Santelle?"

And just like that, with just two words, has me flying once more. Takes me higher as I lift my gaze to meet his. Shivering on a breeze of awakening as I absorb the regal angles of his face, contrasted by the tumble of his dark-gold hair and the contemplative indents of his dimples.

"Are you all right?"

I feel my mouth open. Know sound of some sort needs to follow. "I..."

"She is *fine*." Vylet's tone is playful but her gaze watchful, installing an invisible tether between Cassian and me with the back-and-forth concentration. As if one is not there already...

"At least, she *will* be," Brooke adds. "Forgive her, Cassian. It's this thing called sunshine. New concept for my sweet little *secran*." She tosses a huff at me and then twirls a hand at the palais. "She's always cooped in that place. Day and night, busy as Cinderella in those dark castle halls."

Jagger snorts while shrugging into a black T-shirt. Tosses one to Cassian. "And what does that make you? The evil stepmother?"

"Dude, I'm a wicked stepsister—in all the best ways."

Vylet masks a giggle behind a hand. The tiny nick in her front lip, betraying the cleft repaired when she was a babe, still makes her insecure when men are near—yes, even Alak, her completely smitten *betranli.* "Corrupting her prince, one day at a time."

"Only when it comes to attending his royal balls."

Jagger and Vy fill the air with their laughs. Yes, I fume again. How can I caution the princess about making comments like that when our friends *reward* her for them? Jagger, now Prince Samsyn's key aide in running the security forces of the kingdom, cannot be expected to know better—but I need more support from Vy.

And maybe I am simply being a toddler at the pool again.

I drop my head, wrestling with the thought.

Until muscled thighs in white pants kneel in front of me. And a hand, powerful and long-fingered, slips over my knee. And another hand, warm and firm, tilts up my chin.

And that stare, dark and majestic, wraps around me again. Into me.

"Out of the cinders, Ella." His murmur is formed of the same perfect velvet. "It's time to live in the light."

Survival mode. Now.

Lungs, inflate.

Heart, keep going.

Survival may be overrated. Extremely. Dear sweet Creator, all I want is the blissful release of giving in to his sensual hunt...

Ugh.

Can I get any stupider? Princes like him do *not* chase backward bumpkins like me. They might pretend to...for a little while. Toy with them. Are perhaps amused by them, until the island novelty wears off and they return to the heights of Mount Olympus—also known as New York City—to bed nymphs and marry goddesses.

And despite that entire diatribe, I bear my gaze just as deeply into his—before rasping ridiculous bumpkin words.

"Maybe I like the dark better."

Stupid. Stupid. Stupid.

I expect more giggles from the girls—but they are busy bantering with Jagger, leaving room for the bubble around Cassian and me to thicken. For the world around us to fall away...

For his nostrils to flare, as if catching my scent.

For his lips to part, as if anticipating a bite into his prey.

For my whole body to quiver, as if wanting to let him...

Through one exquisite moment.

Another.

Before being ripped from our reverie by a hand at my elbow. Twisting in, issuing a silent command to get on my feet. I obey before looking, for that grip belongs to just one person in my world—the sole person I expect least right now...and dread most.

"*Paipanne.*" My dutiful murmur is a thread of disguise. Surely he can see every illicit thought that has been possessing my mind and body.

"Mishella," he levels from between tight teeth.

Once more this afternoon, my throat convulses on a dry gulp. *He has seen.* Creator help me.

"High Councilman Santelle." Cassian's tone comes as a surreal interjection. He is not a stupid man. Surely he sees how Father's quiet fury wrings the joy from the air, though he smiles as if exchanging niceties about the weather. "What a pleasant surprise. Thought I'd have to wait for the pleasure of greetings until this evening."

My nerves flee. No. *Wrong.* They double. Ice in one's veins is tricky that way. "Th-This evening?" I dare a glance up at him, forcing my features to neutrality—not an easy task when the wind plays with the edges of his hair and molds his T-shirt against the steely planes of his pectorals.

"Yes." Father's tone modulates to match Cassian's—on the surface. Likely, nobody but Vy and I detect its lingering tension. "It is Mr. Court's last evening on the island, and your *maimanne* thought he might be tiring of the rich *palais* food. He and his retinue shall be dining with us at seven."

"I—I did not know."

"Because you were dressed and out the door before we could tell you this morning."

"And you must be so proud." Vylet slices out the statement before Father can issue another accusation. If I am not tempted to kiss her feet for that, her finishing look is the decider. Few are experts at sweet-but-deadly like my rule-breaking friend.

"I'll back that up," Brooke adjoins. "Your daughter works harder than anyone I know, High Councilman. My life would be a mess without her."

Paipanne colors. A little. "You are too kind, Highness." Dips his head with a thin smile. It assures me little, for his initial agenda, whatever that is, lingers in his steel-gray eyes. "Her maimanne and I are certainly proud of her. On that note, I must have needs to 'borrow' her for a moment. About tonight, you know."

"Of course." The distrust in Brooke's eyes cannot be missed from a hundred feet away, but I sneak a reassuring nod in her direction. Father will not be able to wreak too much damage right here, without all of them watching and noticing. He will restrict the blows to verbal form only; I am sure of it.

And to that, I am well accustomed by now.

CASSIAN

The craving is as shocking as it is sudden.

But sure enough, I long to smash in every inch of Fortin Santelle's self-righteous face.

Why not? He's an ass.

But you've known that from the beginning.

Still, he's the ass willing to vouch for *my* ass with the decision-makers about Arcadia's new infrastructure needs. So yes, I'm conflicted. But...perhaps this has nothing to do with Mishella. Not really. I'm just trying to reconcile doing business with a rung-grabbing bastard. Replacing my discomfort about a future in professional bed with the man by breaking— translation: snapping in half—one of my own hard-and-fast rules. Pushing my nose into his personal affairs. Actually caring about the fact that he treats his own daughter like a puppy to be disciplined.

Stay out of it. Personal ties become business pigsties. Didn't you learn that the hard way? And you haven't dealt with thousands like him before? Even the man you once called father-in-law?

A huff escapes me, thick with relief. At least now I have an explanation. *Displaced emotions, courtesy of the shit storm known as old baggage.* It makes sense—meaning now I can compartmentalize and cope.

Until I look once again at her.

Mishella.

My little Ella.

The words embed into my psyche like diamonds stirred into concrete. She has changed the structure of my being. But how the *hell*? I've seen her exactly six times in the last three days, including what was supposed to be a "casual" welcome reception at the palais but turned into the cataclysm of my first sight of her—and I remember every moment of every encounter since. Even just passing *hellos* with her make it happen all over again—the world fading away, the senses captivated by her—and just like that, my interest is amplified in the island girl with hair like spun gold and eyes like a toy store collector doll.

Interest?

No. I'm not "interested" in her.

I'm fascinated by her. Entranced. Maybe a little obsessed. Maybe a lot more than that. Worse, I have no idea how to explain it—which should scare the living fuck out of me but doesn't.

She feels...right. Secure. Even safe. Yet she's the most exhilarating adventure of my life, a high-wire walk with a view of the entire world.

Just don't look down.

"Christ." I grit it to myself while bending down, retying a perfectly secure shoelace. It's a quick fix; I can keep eyes locked on Fortin and her but hide the growing erection she has inspired.

Yeah. *Inspired.*

What was the word Samsyn used with me last night after dinner, when describing how he'd felt the moment he met his Brooke? It was an Arcadian phrase, unique in its blend of Turkish and French influences...

Soursedias.

Yeah. That. It's goddamn perfect, coming close enough to even the English word for what that woman has done to me.

Sorcery.

Yeah. That has to be it. She's an island enchantress,

empowered by the Arcadian spirits to wrap my mind, soul, and body in a searing, clinging erotic spell. And fuck, is it working. I want to give in to the rest of it, just to know how high and hot she'd take me...

And how far I'd take her. Claim her.

How greatly would her gorgeous innocence change... transformed by lust? How much wider could I make those big blue eyes? What would her pretty bow lips look like, formed into an O of raw desire? What would her refined voice sound like, panting in the spasms of a mindless orgasm?

I break a shoelace.

Snap back to reality.

I have to get off this damn island.

It will happen—first thing tomorrow morning. I'll wrap up the talks with Santelle tonight—not looking in his daughter's direction while doing so—and then tell Mark and his crew I want the plane ready by daybreak. That'll allow time to check numbers in the foreign markets, call my key project managers in New York, and then get out of here before Mishella Santelle can weave any more wonderful witchery into my willing soul.

Witchery.

Who the fuck am I kidding?

She's not a witch. Fairy, maybe. Perhaps an angel, or a mermaid given legs. The certainty hits harder as I stare at her again. She holds herself as regally as any of those, even as her father continues quietly berating her—I cannot label it anything else, if the expression on his face is to be believed— and even in how she sways after he pivots, heading back inside.

But only one sway.

After that, she returns to the queenly stance, holding it despite the wounds Fortin has inflicted. Not physical cuts, but damage just as torturous to bear. Somehow she does, returning to the table with astounding composure. Keeping her shit together even while Brooke and Vylet peal with laughter at some joke from Jagger.

For a moment, I am incensed. How can her two closest friends not see her pain?

Realization. Massive. Maybe *she* doesn't want to see it.

An answer I'll likely never have—and shouldn't want to. Rescuing knight, I sure as hell am not. Repulsive giant in the clouds? *There's* the fit.

And it is well past time for me to climb back up the beanstalk. To remember that counting beans is the only magic left in my life now. No more turns at sorcery. I've had my turn at that shit already. Sucked up my life's ration of magic. Neither of them exists for me anymore.

There's only tonight's dinner to get through first. With the sorceress and her family.

God fucking help me.

CHAPTER TWO

MISHELLA

"Hold. Still."

Though Mother murmurs the words, the command in them is as clear as the directives Father growled at me this afternoon.

Know your place, girl—and stay in it.

Know your purpose, daughter—and stick to it.

I struggle not to wince as she stabs another pin into the bun atop my head. Three pins later, she grunts softly: an approving sound. "Better."

Translation: I look as nondescript as a push-pin. Perfectly acceptable, as far as I am concerned. I have even assisted the effort, selecting a basic black sheath with a demure square neckline and a mid-calf hem. My low heels imbue the ensemble with a tiny stab of class—enough to honor my paipanne without disgracing him—which I apparently accomplished by "fawning" over Cassian Court this afternoon.

With effort, I control the color threatening to invade my cheeks again. I do not dare give Mother any more fuel for her irked fire, which has only increased in the months since I chose to stay on as Brooke's secran. She and Paipanne barely understood my enthusiasm about the position when Brooke had been *queen*; now that she is a mere princess again, my decision is seen as close to walking the streets a whore.

At first, the dichotomy puzzled me. In the palais, I was happy, productive, and certainly protected. But one day, a conversation with Vy shifted my view.

This is not a matter of controlling your virtue, Shella-bean. It is a matter of controlling you.

I'd scoffed, even gotten defensive with Vy, refusing to see my own parents in that light—but more and more evidence has surfaced to support the assertion. Incidents and attitudes I've ignored before, perhaps written off as their love expressed in the only way they knew how...but if that were the case, why does it manifest in that form only with me? How is Saynt so different—or has he received the same pressure since Father and Mother pushed for an early end to his school studies, followed by immediate entry into Arcadian military training? At this rate, he will surely be an officer within a few years—though even that timing does not seem swift enough for them.

But there is no chance to steal away for *that* intimate sibling chat tonight, in light of the events planned down to the second. In that regard, I have an easier assignment than Saynt—a truth Mother reminds me of now, meeting my gaze in the mirror.

"Just cocktails and dinner, hmm?" She arches brows in subtle expectation. "Neither of us needs the fat calories in dessert, anyway."

"Of course, Maim—"

I am interrupted by my own astonishment, when she reaches into my jewelry box and withdraws the amethyst drops from my last birthday. My brows lower. The gemstones are not the plain pearls I would have predicted as her preference—and honestly, they make me squirm a little. They are beautiful but entirely too bright. They are—

"The perfect touch." Like the direction on my hair, it is an order, not a suggestion. She finishes it by holding them against my ears. "Ahhh, yes. Definitely. Perhaps you can talk about how they were passed between each generation in our family... to celebrate our prosperity."

I lower my gaze. It is a sweet story—if only a word of it were true. But Father and Mother are not above "sliding" on the small facts to justify larger gains. As far back as three years ago, before the crown of Arcadia shifted and Evrest Cimarron officially reopened the island to the outside world, they saw Arcadia's future as a major player on the world economy's stage—and did not miss a chance to seize the opportunities from it. A *single* chance. As a result, they have become nothing short of obsessed with the Santelle family holding major strings in the new Arcadian economy.

Now, Saynt and I are expected to shovel into that locomotive too—and long-gone are the days when we were given any preference about our contributions. Saynt is learning to face our enemies, even take a bullet, for the family name. And I'll learn to spread my legs for the man they point me toward.

And oh, yes—to keep my mouth shut on everything but rehearsed lines until then.

Like the propaganda about my earrings.

"I—I shall try." I add a game smile at Maimanne for effect. She does not have to know that just the idea of lying to Cassian sits on my stomach like rotting fish. It feels too close to lying to myself.

The flash of revelation bursts another into life.

Cassian. When he is near, I somehow feel closer to... myself.

To parts of myself beyond "the physical obvis," as Vy would call them. Things far past the racing blood, the lightning nerves, the throbbing womb...

Things that are even better.

Things of wonder.

Anticipation.

Feelings brand-new, tied to desires as old as the ancients.

Needs I have to lock away. *Now.*

Stuff into a place deep inside, as firmly as I seal my pearls back into my jewelry box. Bury deep beneath my gaze, glittering too brightly from the mirror as I secure the amethysts on my ears. Conceal behind my face, lashed into serenity, as Maimanne tilts a last look from the doorway. *That will do,* her eyes seem to say—the closest thing I shall receive in the way of praise.

"That will do." I repeat it to my reflection, fighting for a shred of its reassurance. Press my clammy hands to my flushed face, praying for an infusion of composure. Beseech the Creator for the strength to get through the next three hours, pretending I feel nothing for the man—and his money—who is so important to our family's future.

Because, despite everything, I love them. And know—pray?—in my deepest heart, that all of Father and Mother's maneuvers are for ultimately for Saynt and me. I can support them without having to lie to Cassian about the earrings—or anything else, for that matter.

Except how I feel about him.

Except how two days and six encounters—not that I am keeping track—have transformed the man from a complete stranger into the very nucleus of my thoughts, center of my heartbeats—

And apparition on my balcony?

"Guuhhh!"

Stealing more slang from Vy is better than surrendering to my first option of a reaction: a throat-razing shriek. As I choke the sound all the way down, I thank the Creator his hair is slicked back from his face, tamed into waves catching the outside lights as he swings over the wrought-iron rail from the bougainvillea trellis he has just scaled. Sweet Creator, *his hair.* As long as I live, I will not forget it. Thick as molten gold, streaked with honey straight from the hive—a dangerous thought for all the dangerous things he makes me feel, especially now...flinging open the balcony's double doors, locking his gaze to mine once more—

And bringing pure fire back to my world.

CASSIAN

Will this woman ever not set me completely on fire?

The question is as mystifying as the one before it: the demand that hounded every inch I just clawed up the goddamn trellis. It went something along the lines of: *you swore you wouldn't look at her tonight, yet now you're scaling a wall in the dark, hoping you've pegged the right bedroom as hers?*

Even if there *are* answers, I care nothing for them. I don't care about much of anything, other than the euphoria of knowing I was right. The pastel and cream décor I glimpsed from the ground is hers—and now she is standing in it, a stark contrast in her classic black dress and shoes. Not a hair on her head breaks free from its bun. The look should bring severity to her face but accomplishes the opposite. Every angle of her impeccable beauty is brought out in bold relief, turning her into something close to fine art. I half expect to look down and see a *Do Not Touch* sign attached to a rope around her waist.

Thank fuck there isn't one.

Because I need to touch. *Now.*

One step. Another. Then a stop, wondering if she'll shy back, like this afternoon...like the wiser one she is in this whole thing. She knows the truth, more than me. She understands that these threads between us can only ever be that. Threads, like cocoon floss. Gossamer. Temporary.

But she doesn't move. Simply closes her eyes as my hand raises. Releases a shaky rasp as I curl fingers over her full, beautiful cheek. Finally whispers words like the faint furrows that crinkle the top of her elegant nose.

"How did you..."

I laugh softly. "Damn lucky guess."

"Why..."

"Do you really have to ask that?"

Her eyes open. She swallows hard. "We cannot do this. Mr. Court, I—"

"And do you really have to call me *that*?"

"We are both supposed to be downstairs—where *you* will complete business with my *father*. This is *not* part of the plan."

"The *plan*?" I slide closer to her. God*damn*, her scent. Her skin exudes something exotic, like island flowers. Her hair, while yanked back with some shiny styling product, betrays hints of jasmine and vanilla. "How do I know it's not?"

As I anticipate, her stare snaps up, full of incensed fire.

"It's a fair question." I half abhor myself for venturing down this path. But as long as we're here... "I need your father's influence on this island, but he needs my money. How do I know he hasn't dangled his daughter to sweeten the deal for himself?"

Tears join her fury. Just a sheen—enough to show me the

threads are about to break. Her hand swings up. Flies back. When it's at full height, I snap a grip around her wrist. Use the hold to circle her around, pinning her to the wall behind her terrace door. The shadows of the corner envelop us, making her gritted teeth glow, setting even more fire in her huge sapphire eyes.

"Damn you." Her syllables are more like sobs. They jab my gut, reaffirming that all my stress about doing business with a jackass is pretty stupid. *Like attracts like.*

It's not a new revelation. But right now it sears like pure acid, and I have to halt the damage—no matter how desperate the measure.

"I'm sorry." All right, maybe I *am* desperate. In the last five years, those words have only left my lips once before—on an occasion I'm determined not to dredge up. Not now. "Sshhh, Ella. *I'm sorry.*"

She huffs through her nose. Several more times. "Let me go."

I concede, despite the harsh twist of my gut.

Unbelievably, she stays put. Lowers her arm into a protective wrap around her waist but doesn't move beyond that.

Like an idiot, I brush fingertips up to her face again.

Like a miracle, she lets me.

"I'm a moron. And I *am* sorry." It's the truth. I hope she can feel it in the pressure of my thumb, slowly tracing the strong line of her jaw. God, she's so warm and smooth. "I'm also trying to make logical sense out of this. Out of...us."

Her laugh is quick—and strangled. "There *is* no 'us.'"

"Oh, there's an *us*." And in another bonehead move, I drag her hand away from her body...sliding it beneath my blue silk tie, against the dress shirt covering my sternum. "You know it as well as I do, Mishella. You feel it too. You feel it...right here... don't you?"

Her lips work against each other. "What I feel does not matter. What *either* of us feels—" She lets her hand drop. Blinks slowly, her lashes shimmering with new salty drops. "I am not free to *feel*, Cassian. You must know that by now. You have spent two days exposed to my father's determination and will. He desires your money but only because it will bring him something greater."

"Power." I could have supplied the answer from a coma. It was the Holy Grail of the elite, a high better than multiple zeroes in a man's bank account. And in the hands of fools— worse, in the hands of arrogant fools—it could end the entire planet.

"And my brother and I...are additional tools in helping him gain that power." She looks down, using her dress as a visual aid in her argument. She has no fucking idea that the staid color and the conservative cut, accented only by the gemstones on her ears, have only stoked my imagination more. It's a battle not to visualize peeling the garment away from her sleek curves, her creamy skin contrasted by the dark fabric... and showcasing the marks of my grip. "I am to be the ultimate prize for the man at court who helps our family rise the highest. Any 'dalliance' before that time, especially with an American investor who was only here for three days, would wag enough tongues to lower his asking price for me."

I don't even try to contain a disgusted growl. "Like a fucking virgin offered to a dragon." When her reply is nothing but extended tension, my head jerks up. "Wait. *Shit.* Because you really *are* still a..." Her eyes confirm it in a second.

God*damn*...her eyes. Those wide blue depths, such a turn-on for me from the start, ignite me to shaking lust now. Openness and honesty, because she *is* open and honest.

And a virgin.

A thought—like so many others that have struck about her—that should horrify the hell out of me.

But doesn't.

Holy hell...just the opposite.

The idea of being the first man to fill her...to bring her to the bliss that will convulse her walls around my cock, make her scream my name as I pump my hot release deep inside her body...

Crap. Shit. Fuck.

You've had enough, sailor. Time to close out the tab and wobble on home.

Somebody needs to tell that to the breathtaking blonde now pushing from the wall and pressing her body against mine, that gaze again betraying so many of her thoughts. At least the ones betraying the exact match of her fantasies to mine.

Crap. Shit. Fuck.

No.

"I want to give it to you, Cassian." She slips her hand up to my neck, working those slender, seeking fingers beneath my shirt. "You know that, yes?"

Hell.

Now she curls her heated touch into the ends of my hair, awkwardly at first, as if she's just learned the move from movies and is shocked that it works...that such a small gesture has pierced my entire body, slicing into my cock—pulsing heavily between our bodies. Her lips part on the sexiest gasp I've ever heard. The flare of her gaze ensues, making my dick swell again.

"Creator's sweet stars," she whispers. "Would it even fit?"

"Holy *fuck*."

It's all I can say—fortunately, all I *have* to say. She opens her mouth before I even descend, an invitation to plunge with every wet, needing inch of my tongue, embedding her taste into me...gifting me with her soft supplication. And goddammit, I take it. Every inch, every drop, every taste I can possibly steal.

Because it's all I'll get to take from her.

All I'll allow myself to take.

Because despite how much I want her, I refuse to ruin her. Refuse to even think of what her life could be like if she is of no use to her father's master plan of Arcadian commercial dominance.

Pathetic bastard.

Will he even listen if I tell him it's a losing track? That he'll attain his goal, only to want something beyond it? *Right.* Shaking a spider in its web often just makes the spider work harder—making life hell for its prey.

With a rough moan, I tear myself from her kiss. On legs that shake, step back from her. Then again. Force my hand into a quivering claw, pulling her grip off my neck. But before I set her fingers completely free, I push my face against her palm and impale her gaze with the unmitigated fire in my own.

"It would fit, sweet Circe."

She smiles, acknowledging the illicit imagery I invoke—but winces, recognizing what I do. We'll never act on the words. "Circe." she finally echoes. "The Greek sorceress? The one who transformed her enemies into animals?"

I answer with a growl into her hand. She tries to hide the answering quiver down her body. Fails miserably.

"But you are not my enemy."

"But you have turned me wild."

Her breath catches. In the exquisite silence that follows, sneaks her tongue between her lips.

"*Cassian.*"

My own name has never brought me more heat, more tension...more arousal. Two syllables, and my whole system is heated by another ten degrees...and my cock now throbs against the plane of her belly.

I groan. She whimpers. But the temptation to shove her back, hike her dress to her waist, and take her right here, against the wall, hits my gritted restraint. This woman isn't just a whim. She's not a fuck-then-flee socialite or remotely close to my other preferred social distraction: haute couture bimbo, sans panties. In my jacket pocket is a phone with hundreds of those women on it, willing to be ready the moment my plane touches down in New York once more.

The thought of it makes me ill.

It will pass—it always does—but as I dip toward her, needing one more taste before giving her up forever, I give in to the illusion that it won't. That Mishella Santelle has pulled a real Circe on me and accomplished the impossible.

Transformed me.

Changed me back into a creature I recognize. A man I respect.

Impossible.

Impossible.

I am so screwed.

CHAPTER THREE

MISHELLA

My eyes itch. My back aches. The indents in my palms are likely permanent by now, considering the hours my fingernails have been digging into them. How many hours, I have no idea. At this point, time has been slammed into the same category as my physical comfort level. Irrelevant.

I sit in a stiff chair in Father's study, scooted forward, hands tucked in my lap, knees at a ninety-degree angle. I focus on my toes, flat against the floor, peeking from beneath my sleep pants. Distractedly, I note how they have changed color through the hours, going bluish at the brink of dawn. Living in Sancti, the warmest part of Arcadia, still means ocean breezes that chill the air at night.

Winds capable of lifting Cassian's hair off his high, straight forehead...

Of teasing that hair into his eyes, changing like ripples across a lagoon with his rising desire...

Of infusing a wild new scent across his skin, so taut and tanned over all the hard ridges of his body...

"*Salpu.*"

Not even whispering the profanity against myself is effective against the relentless images of him. And maybe, as awful as the torture is, it is for the best. The pictures are all I will have now.

He is gone.

And I am a selfish salpu for lamenting the bizarre sense of loss in my heart, when so much more has walked out the door with him.

New memories assault, making me grimace. That moment, having let down my hair and climbed into bed, when the door of my chamber burst open...and then my gape when Father filled the portal. Luckily, the curse I had prepared for Saynt was not yet at my lips. I had expected nobody else, since Mother retired to her own quarters after we bid good night to Father and Cassian, immediately following dinner. I had not diverted from acceptable decorum during the meal, despite the yearning to do exactly that—cheese soup, crème fraiche, and stuffed chicken breast gained new meaning when one dined across the table from Cassian Court's intense gaze—but when Father stormed in, rage mottling his face, I discerned the awful truth before he spat it.

Did I not *tell you, two damn days ago, not to throw yourself at the man like a common* rospute? *Do you know what you have done, Mishella? Do you know what you have ruined?*

"Tell me again." Mother's mandate jerks me back to the present—though it is no less agonizing than the flashback. "Word for word, Fortin—what Court said before he left, and when."

Father growls. "I do not fathom how this will—"

"Tell. Me. Again."

"*Woman.*"

"*Husband.*" She jerks the edges of her dressing robe tighter. Firms her stance. She doesn't need to say more. Even with a bare face and tangled hair, etched in the unforgiving gray of early morning, Selyna Santelle's golden beauty arrests a whole room.

Suddenly—strangely—I feel sorry for her. She and Father are children of equally ambitious court schemers who married them off for political gain. For many years now, it has been plain that little connects them but a mutual drive for more. And, I suppose, Saynt and me. They love us, in their bizarre way—which might be the only way they know how.

"He is likely preparing his plane for takeoff as we speak," she persists with the same steely calm. "So if I am to help with salvaging the damage"—a glance in my direction gives chilling clarity about her definition of *damage*—"I must visualize it again. He said he was 'unable' to commit to the agreement 'as is'?"

"Yes," Father bites out.

"Not that he refused the terms outright?"

"He said what he said, Selyna. I did not have time to dally with semantics."

Mother waves a hand like his snarl is a persistent fly. "But *he* took the time to issue the last of it? It was issued in the parlor, not tossed over his shoulder in the front drive, on his way out?"

Father expels a breath. Finally mutters, "Yes. In the parlor. After he turned down cigars, had *one* bite of the trifle, and excused himself to take a discreet shit."

Mother cocks her head. "And you are certain that was it?"

"Certain what was what?"

"The shit. That was what he excused himself for?"

Exhaustion. Shock. *Not* the best combination for containing frantic laughter. A tight choke helps me at the last minute. Is there any ground forbidden in the path of their ambition?

Father's loose shrug confirms the answer. "I gathered so,"

he mutters. "I very well did not listen at the door, though he was gone long enough, so I assumed..."

He trails off with a tense scowl—though it has nothing to do with spying on Cassian's bathroom business. *Assumed.* The word alone implies one of their cardinal sins, as bad as laziness or murder. In this case, it brings just as heinous an outcome— if I correctly interpret the messages beneath their extended, silent exchange...

What if he wasn't spending the time on that *private matter? What if he went to the bathroom for other reasons—such as the chance for second thoughts? Why has he backed out of signing the contract so suddenly?*

No answers of logic or comfort come forth.

The only thing that has changed in the last four months, since Father and Cassian first communicated about this deal, has been—

Me.

I can peg the millisecond my parents reach the same conclusion. My head jerks down as theirs swing around, though that helps not in battling the weight of their scrutiny.

I want to cease breathing. Not an exaggeration. Every breath I take is a sharp slice between my ribs; like the air itself is contaminated by their disappointment—and disgust.

They know.

I have been circling the ugly words, unwilling to accept them, but now they sting as sharply as the cold on my feet and throb as hard as the pain behind my eyes. I drop my gaze to the floor. Wish for a way of lasering an escape hole through the polished wood.

Am I supposed to say something now? What on earth do they expect?

But I know the answer to that already.

It is me. I am the one who derailed it all. Who ruined any respect he had for our family by flirting with him, making stupid eyes at him. Letting him into my bedroom...and letting him do other things there.

And Creator help me, I liked it.

A lot.

And I made him like it.

At least I think *I did.*

Sweet Creator...*did* he like it? And why am I stopping to even wonder about it? Or to care?

But I do. If hell takes me for it, then so be it. My virginity is still pristine, and I shall never again see the man who tempted me to change that, so I cling to the memories of the feelings... all the passionate, exquisite perfection of those moments with him. It is shameless and selfish, and for one sublime moment, *I do not care.* For a collection of perfect breaths, I am again simply a woman letting a man climb up her balcony and then kiss her senseless...render her breathless...arouse her to that perfect place called *mindless...*

All too soon, it is over.

With the stiffness in Father's shoulders, as he abruptly turns away.

With Mother's censuring glance, before she rises like an empress. "What happened after that? When Court returned from the *tuvalette?*"

A blush attacks. The Arcadian word makes the subject *sound* prettier, though the gritty reality remains. And the guilt. Always the guilt. While I hate their bald zeal on so many levels, I crave their parental pride and approval. My flirtations with Cassian did go too far—perhaps the "romantic" breach into my room was even his way of testing my character—making my overnight moping about it even more pathetic. And how many times have I replayed his kiss in my mind, shamelessly using it to keep myself awake, while my parents watched their plans vanish like a sandcastle under a wave?

In Vy's terms, I suck as a human being.

In Brooke's terms, *maybe you've earned the suckage, girlfriend.*

Father gets up. Walks to his desk. Slumps into the chair behind it before drumming impatient fingers atop the unsigned contract in front of him. "He did not say much more than that," he finally states. "'Unable to commit.' Those were his exact words. Then he said he would be 'taking some matters into advisement' and would 'be in touch soon.'"

Not much is different than the first twelve times he has told it—but this time, the words click differently. I jerk up my head to look directly at him—a penance I have avoided for the last six hours. Crazily—perhaps insanely—it drives words to my lips too.

"'Be in touch,'" I echo. "That is not a full *no*...right?"

Father does not answer. His features are fixed, frozen and dispassionate, as Mother answers me instead—by digging a scalding grip into my ear. I gasp in place of a scream. The woman has perfected ear twisting to such an art, Saynt still bears a tear at the back of his lobe from the day he skipped school as a boy.

"Stand. Up," she seethes. "You know nothing of these matters, girl—and now you will admit that as you apologize to your father, who *might* be able to salvage the mess you have made of this."

A thousand needles stab the backs of my eyes. I grit them back while trying to nod, but her fingers feel sewn to my flesh.

Her grip is unyielding. And maybe it *is* what I need. Maybe I am just a stupid girl, playing with fire much too golden, beautiful, and hot for me to ever handle safely. Maybe, Creator help us, my lustful idiocy has not torched everything they have worked for. Maybe Father *can* fix it...if I get out of his way. If I am humble and prove it by being truly sorry.

It feels right, this simple acceptance of their truth...of my fate. Fighting it, doubting them...it has been exhilarating and exciting—and exhausting. Now a sad peace sets in, like a field mouse surrendering to a hawk's grip, simply letting the end happen—

Until Maimanne jerks to a stop.

I save my ear by skidding short with her—or have my senses been my saviors, sizzling from the blast of new electricity on the air?

Oh...my.

Every neuron in my body is fried from it, letting the energy in—recognizing it at once.

Knowing *him* at once.

By the Creator.

He has returned.

But my joy is instantly shadowed—by mortification. Cassian Court has come back—to find me being led around by the ear, clad in nothing but my sleepwear. And there go any lingering thoughts for him, at least the good ones, about our passion last night...

Though all I behold on his face right now is...

Fury.

Taut, defined, and clear, all across his perfect, noble features...

And all directed at Mother.

"Let her go."

I blink. Again. Yes, the words have emanated from *him*—inducing Maimanne's incredulous sputter. Then her forced, tinkling laugh. "Ahhh, Mr. Court! What a delightful surprise. Did you have to let *yourself* in? I apologize; good help is so hard to find on this tiny island, and we were not aware you would be—"

"Mistress Santelle." Every syllable is a scimitar, bleeding even her conjured civility from the air. "What *wasn't* I clear about?"

He steps over, readjusting a black messenger bag over his right shoulder, making me wonder if there's a gun stowed inside. He looks like a man intent on drawing a firearm—and using it.

I shiver, boldly afraid. Then gasp, blatantly stunned.

Dear *Creator*. Has the fear...aroused me?

Though Mother drops her hold, everything still feels surreal. Never has a man said such things on my behalf...been so *enraged* on my behalf. Or is that it at all? What in Creator's name is going on? Cassian's energy is so different now. While he has changed into more relaxed attire—a white cable-knit sweater and tailored khaki slacks—his demeanor is more high protocol than at any court event I have attended. And I have been to *many*.

The same curiosity governs Father's face as he rises. "Cassian." His extended hand is given a mechanical shake in return. "To what do we owe the pleasure of your return?"

One of Cassian's tawny brows hikes up—which, of course, makes more of me quiver. Even the forbidden parts. "You weren't expecting me to?"

"In a word," Father rejoins, "no."

Bizarrely, *that* nicks Cassian's armor. He chuffs without humor. "Then you've misread the business, Fortin. In this case, luckily, it hasn't cost you the business too."

My jaw almost plummets. No one has ever dared this kind of thing with Father. Reproving Fortin Santelle like this, even disguised as "casual" conversation, would drop jaws up and down the halls of the palais. Father has even struck servants for less.

But the look on Cassian's face...as if he is nearly *enjoying* this...

My nerve endings go icy. By the powers...I'm actually afraid for him.

Until a new recognition sets in.

Father cannot call on a single recourse against this man. Before him stands Cassian Court: an equal individual. A leader from the most cutthroat kingdom on earth. New York City.

My lungs clutch. What will Paipanne say? Do?

"Ah. So we still have business?" His desperation is hidden beneath the diffidence, but Cassian sees through it...is utterly beautiful about it. I am only aware of movie stars through pictures Vylet brings up on her computer—when the Arcadian internet chooses to function—but I easily imagine the man as the chiseled star of a high-stakes spy thriller, detecting every weakness in his opponent in the space of a glance.

Cassian himself only fuels that vision—perhaps even enhances it, with a study of Father that reminds me of straight-from-the-mine emeralds. He is...breathtaking. "I said I needed to take advisement, not my complete leave."

Father stiffens again. "You also said you could not sign the agreement."

"I said I couldn't sign *that* agreement." Out from the

messenger bag, in his impossibly long fingers, comes a sheaf of papers. "This one, I'll sign."

Mother snags the air with a caught breath. Father balances her, barely flinching. But his gaze goes to work, descending in another silent assessment of Cassian...searching for weakness. He will be out of luck. Cassian remains a perfect, unreadable wall: a hotter, steelier version of Jason Bourne, Jack Ryan, Ethan Hunt, and all their friends put together. He stands tall and determined, legs braced in a solid *A*, locking hands firmly as soon as Father takes the papers...appearing like he has all the time in the world to wait for feedback.

It does not take nearly that long.

Less than a dozen seconds, to be exact.

Which has to be a record for transforming my father from practiced deal broker into stunned gaper.

"We discussed a loan of twenty million."

"Correct," Cassian replies.

"This offer is for twice that."

"Also correct."

Maimanne gasps again. I join her. *Forty million dollars? Am I doing the math correctly?* I cannot be certain, since every cell in my brain is short-circuited.

"And you cut the interest rate...in half."

As Mother and I now struggle against fish gawks, Cassian's face is unchanged. "Also correct," he states.

"As well as a finder's fee for any additional opportunities in Arcadia that arise within the next year."

"Yes."

I almost beg Mother to pinch my ear again—or anything else, to ensure this is not a dream. The only thing holding me back: the look on Father's face. His gape is gone, replaced by a troubled scowl—shot at me and then Cassian, in that order.

My heartbeat stutters all over again. By the powers, what have I done now? More precisely, what kind of concessions has Cassian demanded in return for this astounding new deal? The contract is practically Faustian—except the devil looks like an angel, moves like a prize fighter, and enthralls like a wizard.

"All for this sole condition?" Father presses.

Mother practically leaps forward. "Accept it! Whatever it is, Fortin, say yes!"

Father looks at her for a long moment. Then once more at me, his gray gaze suddenly hazy—like that of a field mouse in a hawk's talons.

"The acceptance is not mine to give."

CASSIAN

"This is insanity."

It's the eighteenth time she's blurted it. Yes, I'm counting—wondering if she'll hit the internal estimation I set during the drive back over here, after having the new contract printed up in one of the palais offices. Somehow, Doyle found a security guard to open one of the rooms for us at four in the morning. Not that I'd ever planned on sleeping, after walking out of here consumed by the proposal now outlined in the pages in her hands.

Proposal.

That's one way of putting it.

In the last half hour, she's come up with quite a few more—though *insanity* is the favorite, as I'd predicted. Doyle—I make a mental note to give him a massive bonus, after the miracles he's pulled to make this happen in less than six hours—clearly has some more for the list. His stare, filled with have-you-lost-it perplexity, burns from the shadows of the wingback in the corner. I don't earn myself a reprieve by jerking my head, motioning him out the door—*not* the one beyond which the Santelles are waiting in suspicious silence. It's the one opening onto a small patio with the morning sun now glittering in a small fountain flanked by padded chairs.

Doyle's eyes narrow tighter.

I nod toward the patio again.

With a grunt, he rises. Fortin has all but ordered him to witness every second of my conversation with Mishella, but we're not going to move past the next "this is insanity" at this rate. The dynamic in the room badly needs to change—and D has to know that too. On paper, the guy is my valet, but that bullshit flies as much as saying the same thing about Kato and the Green Hornet. Doyle and I finish thoughts, sentences, and cheeseburgers for each other. He's the closest thing I have to a sibling. At least one who's alive.

As soon as D steps outside, my theory proves out. A rush of relieved breath leaves Mishella.

Just as rapidly, she pulls one back in.

Wheels on me so fast, her loose hair tumbles over her shoulder...

And her breasts pucker beneath her pink sleep shirt.

She's so fucking sexy, I can barely think.

But I must. Force myself to, with willpower I'm now grateful to have fortified over the years...the only thing riveting me in place as blood rushes to stupid places in my body.

"This is insanity!"

So much for theories.

"You must know that," she continues, once more pacing the length of the room. "You—you *have* to know that."

I can reply right away—I actually *have* known that since leaving this mansion the first time—but I don't. Instead I lean against her father's desk, bracing hands to the wood at my sides, giving her the full thrust of my gaze, the full recognition of my intent...

The full truth of my spirit.

"It feels more crazy to think of leaving without you."

It's a bomb drop even to me, but I don't try to mitigate the blast. I don't want to. The shrapnel cuts in, and I let it. I welcome the blood; the sensation that I'm watching my heart fall on the floor. For a second, I simply revel in watching it pump. For so many years, I've had my doubts.

I'm braced for the twentieth reference to lunacy, but she turns instead, brow tightly knitted. In a rasp, she asks, "Why?"

I quirk a small smile. "After the last two days, do you really have to ask? Wait." I push up, a move easily carrying me into the steps remaining between us. "After last *night*, do you have to ask?"

She tilts her head up. I'm certain she must hear the thunder in my chest, now so close to her stunning face, as I take in her flash of joy. She hasn't just remembered what happened in her bedroom. She's relived it as many times as I have.

Which doubles my confusion about the new mask she slams down over that bliss. "Cassian—"

"Ella." Yes, I use the name intentionally. With just as much purpose, grip her by both elbows. I don't shirk the hold, even when she stiffens against it.

"Why do you insist on calling me that?"

"Why do you insist on pretending you don't like it?" When

she relents, just for a moment, I seize the chance to move an inch closer. Nearly fitting our bodies against each other... "Why do you insist on acting like you're not pleased with my revised proposal to your father?"

"Proposal." She twists both arms free, stumbling back. "*That* is what you have titled it?" The arms fold back in. She spits a bitter laugh. "And I thought Arcadia had been missing out on so many miracles of the modern world. But if buying a human being is still simply relegated to a piece of paper—"

"Okay, slow down." I half-expected her to go here. I *didn't* expect the vehemence with which she'd do it—or the pain in her eyes as she did. "Nobody is getting 'bought,' Mishella."

"Right," she retorts. "*Désonnum*. So sorry. My big bad. You do not wish to purchase; you simply want to rent."

"What?" I want to be angry, but shock makes that impossible. "Where do you get—"

"Six months." She sweeps a hand toward the contract. "I have that correct, yes? Is it not all completely spelled out in your pretty papers? You agree to invest forty million dollars in Arcadian entities recommended by my father, in exchange for getting to have me on call to you for the next six months."

A band of pain clamps my head. I step back before snarling, "Not *on call*." It's no less crude than her inflection.

"Oh?" One of her hands hitches to a hip. "What, then? Forty million dollars' worth of *companionship*? A 'plus one' for social affairs? A movie buddy? A dog trainer?"

One side of my mouth kicks up again. "You want a dog?"

Her eyes widen. I swear that inside, she's just regressed to the age of six. "Do—do you have one?"

"I can get you one."

The six-year-old disappears. The woman is back, head

tilting, going for what she perceives to be cynicism. "Cassian, are you seriously saying you expect me to return to New York with you...and not fuck you?"

Well, *hell.*

I'd anticipated that question too—*hello, obvious*—just not those words for it. And *those* words, flowing in *her* musical voice...what they instantly do to me...

Damn. *Damn.*

Everything in my body tightens. The skin around my cock does *not* get a free pass. The fucker just got charged double fare, and he's not happy about it. The insult to the injury: that tiny tick of her auburn eyebrows, which might as well be fist pumps in some unseen boxing match to which she's challenged me.

Okay, sweetheart. You take that victory dance. I'll wait riiiight here.

I've never looked forward more to surging off the ropes.

And I do.

One unwavering step...two...and then I'm right back next to her, screwing propriety, manners, and personal space, molding our bodies exactly as they'd been in the recesses of her bedroom. Just as intoxicating as those shadows is the Arcadian morning sun, surrounding us...warming her lips for a kiss I long to brand on her, into her, through her. But I don't. I lean until only the tips of our mouths touch, enlivening those areas so exposed yet so erotic, making us breathe together— me out, her in, then reversed—until she shudders harder than the motes in the rays around us.

"Mishella."

Her eyes drag open. Just a little. "Hmmm?" Then pop wide as I drop both hands around her ass. Wider as I jerk her body tighter against mine.

"You're not going to fuck me in New York."

"I—" For a moment, before she attempts to hide it, she looks dejected. "I'm not?"

"*I'm* going to fuck *you.*"

She swallows. "Oh." Pulls in trembling air. "Um...*oh.*"

I roll my hips, making sure the layers of our clothes don't cushion the erect enforcer of my meaning. Complete backfire. My dick rails it at me, screaming to be set free in the hot, soft valley between her lush thighs. Somehow, I'm still able to get words out. Hoarsely.

"You know what else?"

"Wh-What else, Cassian?"

"You're going to beg me for it."

Bigger gape. So goddamn captivating. I could get lost in every facet of her huge sapphire eyes. "I'm—*oh.*"

Her helpless rasp warms my neck. The heat from it reverberates, echoing along my muscles and tendons, my blood vessels and skin cells, an assault of demand to give her a preview of exactly what I'm talking about. But another element shimmers in her breath...and now in the gaze she lifts at me.

She's still afraid.

And I refuse to push her...until she's afraid of only the good things.

With gritted effort, I loosen my hold and step away. My hand finds one of hers. I lead her over to the wingback Doyle was moping from. She looks much better in the thing, the golden tumble of her hair contrasted by the dark leather. Her posture is pristine, though her gaze doesn't miss an inch of my actions. Christ, she's beautiful. My misplaced Cinderella, complete with the princess pink PJs.

"All right," I state, hunkering before her. "Perhaps we

should step back."

Her stare clouds. "But you just made me sit."

I quell a chuckle through supreme effort. Lift an indulgent smile—*not* an effort at all. "Just an American expression, *favori.*"

The Arcadian endearment is clearly a surprise—but her small smile confirms it's a pleasant one. "What does it mean?"

"That we should look at this with the body parts above our necks."

She flushes. "A wise idea." Nods. "And a good term. I shall have to journal it."

More of my chest warms. Her journals—one of the first things that fascinated me about her, after recovering from the blow of her beauty—are so much a part of her, it's strange seeing her without one. She keeps them about everything, as if afraid facts will slip into nothingness if she doesn't harness them on paper.

Or maybe they're tangible proof that she controls *something* in her world.

I tuck away the observation—and my anger from it—to the *Deal With This Later* file. Just like the surges I battled during dinner last night, when once more she was spoken to like a dog to be curbed, the emotion has no place or use here. Instead I focus on the gentle trust in her grip, while softly prompting, "You remember the most important point, don't you?"

She nods like a child pulling up multiplication tables. "There are three signature lines on the new contract. Yours, Father's, and mine. The contract is not valid without my agreement."

"Which means what?"

"Which means the ultimate choice about this is mine."

"Good."

My voice is serrated, and I don't hide it. God help me, even her earnestness is a turn-on. I'm a bastard for fantasizing about what it could be when used for carnal purposes, but my guilt is balanced by conviction. She's the pure air my life has needed for so long. The fresh start I didn't even know I craved, until two days ago.

"What else?" I manage to continue. She fidgets a little. Then more. How the hell has a woman with such light been forced to hide it so thoroughly? "Ella, it's all right. It's just us. I'm listening."

I'll always listen.

"This—this is not you 'buying' me," she finally mumbles.

I let my hands slip free. Lean back on my haunches, sensing she needs the distance. "But you don't believe that."

Her lips purse. "It is a nonnegotiable part of the contract, Cassian. What would you have me believe?"

I firm my own features. It's the hardest goddamn thing to do around her, screwing on my "business" brain, but I cinch the fucker tight and go on, "Because your father would be open to considering the courtship of an American otherwise?"

"You underestimate my father's open-mindedness when money is part of the equation."

"I don't underestimate it one bit. But for all intents and purposes, at least in his eyes, I'll be carrying you off and then ruining you." I have to force the next words out. "Making your involvement an 'option' gives him an opening for sneaky bullshit. I wouldn't put it past him to double-dip on this opportunity."

Her nose crinkles. "I do not understand. Double...dip?"

"He'll take my money but still sell off your greatest asset to some horny Arcadian courtier who's stupid enough to believe some made-up line about your absence, like you've been on the other side of the island on a 'research trip' for Brooke." I raise both brows. "There are men that gullible in the Arcadian court, Ella. If *I* can discern that after two days here—"

"I know, I know." Her eyes squeeze shut. "Your assessment is—" A wince takes over. "Correct," she finally concludes. "You are...correct."

More than she wants me to be. The slew of truths has stabbed her, as I knew it would—but this is why I've ordered her parents from the room. If they were still here, she wouldn't feel safe to speak this honestly. "My 'greatest asset,'" she finally echoes, blinking at me with aching eyes. "Is that what you are after too, then? Have all the shops on Fifth Avenue run out of shiny virgins, that you have seized the chance to snap one up as a souvenir from Arcadia?"

Her defiance marks each word, but she ends with a ragged inhalation—already expecting my righteous fury. *Silly, sad, heartbreaking woman.* If she only knew that *righteous* and I have never claimed to remotely know each other—such an abiding truth, her question was one of my first considerations when drafting the new contract.

Battling the urge to yank her close, I settle for locking her in by leveling our gazes. "Ella, if I'd met you here as a hooker in the Sancti marketplace, it wouldn't have mattered." I stop for a second, considering that. "Though I'd likely be on my knees in your pimp's living room instead of here..."

"Having an easier time of it."

We laugh at her finishing my thought. We sigh because that feels as natural—and as exhilarating and as intense—as the rest of what has happened between us. We sober because the enormity of it hits again too. The mutual recognition that if this is what everything feels like after two days, I shouldn't be pushing fate's favor by forging a contract for six months.

Six months.

Not. Nearly. Enough.

I shove aside the sentimental bullshit. *It's enough, you mooning ass.* Long enough to get my fill of her but not so long that I tire of her. More importantly, not long enough for her to start tugging at the threads...asking all the wrong questions...

The threads don't get tugged.

The secrets *don't* get revealed.

It's for the best, no matter how hard she gets my cock or complete she makes my spirit. In the tapestry of her life, I'll become just a thread as well. *The way it should be.* The lover who took her virginity but gave her a bigger gift in return.

Her freedom.

And there's the ultimate ace card in my deck.

The one element she cannot obtain on her own...just six months within her grasp. I watch her start to understand it, her eyes eagerly glittering, even before I speak again.

"Now tell me the third stipulation, Ella. I need to know you understand it."

She responds inside a beat. Imagine that.

"After six months, I shall return to Arcadia. My job as Brooke's *secran* will be returned to me...and I shall be free to wed a man of my choosing, for whatever reasons I deem acceptable." An incredulous smile flows over her lips. "Even for love."

"Yeah. Even for love."

I fight to ignore how good it feels to hear her say it.

And how fucked-up it feels to force my lips around the same words.

And how confusing it is to watch shadows invade her gaze again.

"Of course...I can also choose not to marry at all." She pulls a corner of her lip under her teeth. Toys with the rivets in the chair's arm. "Perhaps...simply...take a string of lovers."

I don't miss how she finishes it. Her surreptitious glance, darted through her tawny lashes, is a cock-grabbing mixture of question and flirtation. Why deny her the show she's looking for? The instant strain through my whole body. The leap of peeved color up my neck, into my face.

She releases her lip—but instantly wets it. Blinks heavily, clearly perplexed again. *Goddammit.* My jealousy is actually turning her on, and she doesn't even realize it. The little sorceress has bewitched *herself.*

Maybe she needs a jolt of clarification. Maybe we both do. Torch to my kerosene.

I surge forward, slamming into her, submerging us in the depth of the chair, mashing our mouths in a burst of passion and heat. Not waiting for permission, I lunge my tongue inside too. Mate it with hers in complete, carnal intent. There's no ambiguity; she knows what I'm thinking: if she signs that contract, the next six months are going to be about purging this from both our systems, in whatever ways it takes. Whatever the fuck *this* is...

Right now, I don't want to explore the options around that answer.

Right now, I push my knees apart, opening a space for myself between her legs. Our crotches slide and thrust; even through our clothes, the fit is perfect.

Right now is for ensuring she receives one message only—with complete clarity.

"Ella..."

"H-Huh?"

"Why don't we focus on you enjoying your *first* lover?"

CHAPTER FOUR

MISHELLA

I blink.

Once more, very slowly—almost wishing everything around me would click into the same speed. That button is *not* working. I am caught one step behind, watching as my worldly possessions roll by, stuffed into three suitcases, down the narrow strip of asphalt Arcadia calls a tarmac.

Is this happening?

This cannot be happening.

I have surely not done this. Agreed to this.

I take it back. I take it back!

The words are so shrill and loud in my head, surely everyone—and I do mean *everyone*—can hear them, even over the revving engines of Cassian's private airplane.

I have never traveled in anything that moves faster than a jeep.

Ohhhhh crap crap crap crap.

I gulp hard. Vylet squeals, her face alight with joy. She is accompanied by Brooke, who wears a smile so wide, she has officially inducted herself as the third member of our "sis-friend-hood." They haul me into a three-way embrace, where our dipped heads form seconds' worth of a private chat room. The two of them do *not* waste the time.

"You know the only reason I'm *even* agreeing to this is because Samsyn and Evrest vouched for this bozo," Brooke asserts.

"And the only reason I agree is because she does."

A giggle spurts out. I am not sure if it is due to sheer nerves, their wonder twins of protectiveness thing, or both, but I am grateful for the respite from decorum. "So you both have reminded me. Repeatedly."

"Good," Brooke volleys. "That means you remember the rest of it too."

"Sure does." Vy hip-bumps me. "Give us the rest of it, Mistress Santelle." When I give nothing but a *psshh*, she nudges harder. "*The rest of it.*"

I squeeze her as hard as I can. She knows I need to be irked in order to fight off the tears. *It is only six months. It is only six months. I can do this. At least I* think *I can.*

"Shella-bean!"

I jump a little before girl-growling—but continue to hold her tight. "If the bozo goes bonzo, I call the sis-friend-hood hotline." That is their nickname for our online video chat room.

Brooke nods in approval. "You call it *any* time, girlfriend. Day or night. Seven hours isn't that huge a time difference."

"Says the girl who has not been roused in the middle of the night by the hotline buzz?" It really *is* one of the most obnoxious sounds I have ever heard—but it can rouse Saynt from a dead sleep, so I know it works.

"Not yet," she jokes back. "Maybe this is our chance to really test it out."

And maybe it should not be.

Why am I going to do this? *How* am I going to do this? I

will be living in a world without them—a world as foreign to me as Antarctica, with but a thousand Arcadian dollars in my purse, three suitcases full of belongings, and the promises of a man I barely know.

No. Also not true.

A man...I *do* know.

A man I have known from the moment our eyes met and our hands joined. As if we had just been two ends of a drawbridge, waiting to be dropped back into place, leading the way back to the castle of us.

A man who, even now, as I dare a glance up, seems to know exactly what I need in this surreal moment.

It is not the strength of his stance, nor the determination in his eyes. They help, but they are not the key.

They are not his nod.

One movement. A sole dip, as forceful as the motors behind him, as clear as the sky into which we are bound, that gives me all the truth of his purpose once more. That infuses me with the bursting belief in it.

That reminds me of exactly what Brooke said, during the hour she and Vy had helped me pack.

I married Samsyn three hours after I was asked, girlfriend— by his freaking brother.

Neither Vylet nor I pointed out that his brother was also her king and that the reason—at the time—was for Arcadian national security. I do not possess even half as good an excuse, but nor am I committing to Cassian Court's ring on my finger. *It is only six months.*

"By the powers," I mutter, solely to myself.

Six. Months.

When I return, it will be to stand as a *maide attendant* for the "real wedding" Brooke and Samysn are starting to plan: a grand double ceremony with Evrest and Camellia's.

When I return, Saynt will be keeping watch over that event—as a full-fledged soldier in the Arcadian Army.

When I return...so much will be different.

Especially me.

I am terrified again. Not even another nod from Cassian fixes it, especially as I turn to my brother, who clenches his jaw and blinks suspiciously shiny eyes. I tug his chestnut hair free from its tie and mess the strands until they're tangled, but that does not prevent the crushing ferocity of his parting hug.

"I took Court outside while you were packing," he says into my ear. "Told him that if he hurts you in *any* way or lets any fucker in that crazy city hurt you, that contract is null and void—and I will come get you myself."

I pull back by a little, not sure how to react. I go for the honesty of my curiosity. "Wh-What did he say?"

"That it would not be necessary." Reluctant grunt. "That he plans on treating you like the treasure you are—and that if you do not feel as such and desire to come home, he will put you on the plane himself, anytime."

I threaten a sisterly smack by narrowing my eyes. His handsome face does not falter. "He really...called me a treasure?"

"Why do you think I am not blocking your way to the stairs?"

I crush him close again. Emotion floods me, and I shake from the force of it. I am a...*treasure*. Not just to the guy who has to feel that way because of genetics, but to the man who looks on, emerald gaze gleaming, the rest of his face seeming like a knight reverently waiting for his lady...

Returning his stare, I smile. In my mental journal, I record the metaphor, for it fits. Knightly passion, while perfect, was never intended to last. What kind of perfection ever was?

Six months is an ideal time limit for perfection.

The conclusion lends me the steel for the last of my goodbyes. Maimanne and Paipanne.

I turn, dutifully ducking my head before them both. Mother is the first to tuck me close, pressing quick kisses to both my temples before scooting back and murmuring, "You are to use that money *only* for emergencies. You have it stowed safely, yes?"

I lift my head. Search for the sheen in her eyes like Saynt's, indicating she's muttering about money to cover deeper emotions and that she worries about me leaving for a city with a population ten times that of our island...

Her eyes are hard as flint.

I suppress my disappointment as Father steps over. Perhaps they have agreed *he* will handle the emotional overtones of the farewell. Makes sense. Mother is not a "public display of affection" type—actually, she is not an advocate of the practice in private either—meaning Paipanne has surely been assigned the parental parting duties.

I lift a new smile at him, giving it an I'm-being-brave-but-do-not-feel-it wobble. He leans over—and bestows the same dual kisses on my forehead, with the same formality as Mother. Tilts my head up so I am impaled by the similar granite of *his* stare.

"Do not disgrace our family."

So this is what a fist in the heart feels like.

I step back, struggling around the blow for breath that needs to come. The pressure surges, jerking my shoulders back and my head up. As I look one last time, I borrow a heavy scoop of stone from both of them—one for my left eye, one for my right.

"Have not a worry, Paipanne. I know exactly what is important to you."

CASSIAN

"What is it?"

The words are out the second I guide her into the leather chair next to mine and then cinch her seatbelt. The syllables are damn near a demand by this point, but maybe that's for the best. Whatever force of fate has spurred my inner caveman for this woman has intensified tenfold by watching her board the plane like a zombie, her steps full of wood and her eyes full of loss.

"*Mishella.*"

Her head jerks up—and for a second, she terrifies me. Her gaze takes me in as if she's been jerked out of a dream. Worse, as if we've never met.

Second thoughts?

Dammit...no.

"What. Is. It?"

Suddenly, she's back—honing her gaze into me as if she wants to laser me open. Pressing fingers to my face and infusing it with the same penetrating force. I battle—in vain—to keep those beams from searing my cock. *Lasered. Game over.* Hasn't it been from the start with her?

"You...really care how I answer that."

She doesn't phrase it as a question, but I hear her bewilderment, responding with a slow nod. I don't want her to stop touching me.

"But that does not matter," she finally murmurs. Expels

a long sigh, as if making room for the fresh infusion of sadness over her lush features. "Just get me out of here. Now. Please."

CHAPTER FIVE

MISHELLA

For a second—perhaps many more than that—I regret letting go of my rage in favor of ogling Cassian like a hormone-drenched teenager. Can I be blamed, after the ferocity of his stare, the press of his lips to my knuckles, and the way he barks, "Wheels up" into a phone in the bulkhead? Just as it has been since we arrived at the airport, every move is about my needs and comfort...

Even now, when a lot of my comfort is beyond his control. *A lot* of it.

With the exception of the juncture of our hands, my whole body twists from the race of my bloodstream, the heave of my lungs, the tripled pumps of my heart. Was I actually congratulating myself on the tarmac for thinking the engines' roar was the scariest part of this "flying" thing? Now, with the whole plane shaking as it gains momentum, faster and faster down the runway, I clamp my eyes shut, grit my teeth, and pray to the Creator I will survive—

"Ella."

How can he sound so gentle, in the middle of such violence?

"*What?*"

"You need to breathe."

I yearn to hurl a glower—but opening my eyes is not a viable option. "No."

"Favori."

"Do *not* speak at me with sweets."

"You mean...try to sweet talk you?"

"Now you *laugh* about it?" The glare cannot be helped. Neither, it appears, can his dimpled grin, making me rip up all my mental bookmarks—even the one I have all but glued to the page marked *Cassian Court: Arrogance in the Air.*

The air.

We are...in the air.

My breath clutches to a brand-new stop—as I watch the runway disappear, giving way to the aqua expanse of the sea. Then a wisp of a cloud. Another.

"Holy shit!"

Cassian laughs from his belly, but I do not care, nearly scrambling over that part of him to gape out the window. A sound escapes me, unlike any I have made before, because it is born of sensations I have never felt before. Fear, yes—but now churned into something beyond. Exhilaration duels with ebullience. Anxiety, but tempered with a new awareness altogether. Something light, like the dandelion seed the plane now feels like. Possibility in the space of a breath.

Is this...freedom?

The knowledge is a crash inside, breaking apart a shell I have never consciously admitted to—but now let myself step from, hatched into something new. Some*one* new. She is a stranger to me, and I long to crawl back right away into the safety of the tiny world behind me, to the security of the tiny girl who lived there.

Who *lived* there.

And I realize...

There is no "taking it back."

I have agreed to let Cassian show me how good those words can be. Signed my name on his paper, giving him the right—and the power—to do so. Power not just over where my body physically goes...but the vistas my mind, soul, and senses are taken to, as well.

And I think an airplane takeoff has been the most terrifying part of my day?

What in Creator's name have I done?

The query makes me tilt my head—toward the man in whose lap I am practically perched. I am not surprised to find Cassian already staring at me. The intensity on his face is another element entirely.

Arrogance in the sky. He is still that—only now, Mr. Confidence is subdued to silence. Perhaps even humbled. The green glass shards in his eyes spike with the crowning truth atop that. *Because of you.*

I have no idea how to answer that...save with one set of words.

"*Merderim*, Cassian Court."

One side of his mouth hitches up. "Thank *you*, Mishella Santelle."

More of the shell shatters.

As more of me steps free, my spirit moves toward the one path in this new world that makes sense...and the perfect, emerald-eyed guide waiting to lead me on it.

My fingers lift to his jaw.

The other side of his mouth raises.

I push my fingers in a little more. Pull tenderly at his jaw.

I want that mouth on mine.

With a ragged grunt of acknowledgment, Cassian obliges.

CASSIAN

How could just a brush of lips be the best fucking kiss of my life?

There are no answers for that.

There are a million answers for that.

My mind implodes on the conflict—the same way it explodes from merely a memory of that sweet, inexplicable touch of her mouth...

Now nearly three hours ago.

I continue gazing at her in sleep, where I fixate on the plush pads that have tossed me into this chaos. Doesn't help a goddamn bit. With Doyle snoozing in the small bedroom at the back of the plane, I'm alone up here with my sorceress— who has me as baffled, bewitched, and just as stunned as I was after kissing her.

And tasting her...

and breathing her in...

then fighting to push her back out.

A lot of good the effort yields me.

She has beaten me.

Good business means admitting when one is defeated, as well as celebrating when one is victorious.

And isn't that the rub?

Mishella Santelle is *not* good business—or so nearly all my teams inform me. Flying all the way to Arcadia, searching for the angles to maneuver Fortin Santelle and *save* money, don't match what I'm returning with: a contract at double the budget and a "houseguest" for the next six months. What the hell else am I supposed to call her? Like the explanation will fly for one second with Prim and Hodge—both of whom I will put off thinking about until we're much closer to home. A "treat" to look forward to, if Doyle's dour looks have been accurate prophesy—and they usually are.

I don't give a fuck.

I would've paid four times as much for her. Been just as glad I had, for the payback of that kiss alone—though karma now carves her pound of flesh right out of my libido.

That kiss.

I crave so much more.

Goddammit, I've paid for it.

No. You've paid for the right to explore this with her, not take it from her. Dial it back, asshole. You've only brought this torture on yourself.

The woman herself helps with the meaning of that final pronoun, sighing sleepily...stretching until her pink sweater set is yanked tightly across her sleek figure. I watch the fabric slide across her breasts, mentally filling in the basic white bra that undoubtedly covers them.

Suddenly, every lace-clad temptress I've been with before is a dim memory behind Mishella's hot-as-fuck take on that Doris Day goodness. Is she wearing matching panties? And is she still so soundly asleep, she won't notice if I try confirming with a peek under her skirt?

Sick. Fuck.

"Mmmm."

While her moan kills off my Peeping Tom, it wakes up my Ready-To-Go Randy. I shift in my seat, adjusting the wood to a more tolerable angle.

Her eyes open halfway and then take me in fully.

"Hey there, little Ella."

She curls a drowsy grin. "Bad princess. I fell asleep in the carriage—even after the prince's kiss."

Hell. She has to mention the kiss. "I'm no prince, Miss Santelle." *Especially after what you've done to my thoughts in the last three hours.*

"Well, thank the Creator." The moment it spills, she clearly can't believe it has. With a dogged shake of her head, she peers out the window. "It is...still light outside."

There's a question in her voice. "Ah. Yes." I follow her gaze, to where the dark-orange rays glint against the plane. "We're chasing the sun—for another hour, at least." Unable to rein back the action, I run a hand down the back of her head—intending to do only that. *Slow the fuck down. You have six months.* But when I pull it back, she chases my touch with her head. Burrows so deeply against my hand she ends up pressed against my chest. After the discernible *click* of her seat belt, the rest of her follows, sitting fully on my lap...

And I sure as hell don't stop her.

"Do you...mind?" She glances up, adorably sheepish. "I can see the sunset better from here."

"And I can see *you* better from here." I let a full grin escape. Goddamn, it feels good. "So it's a win-win."

I hope for a smile in return, perhaps even one inviting a new kiss, but her nose crinkles and her gaze remains somber. "This decision...the new contract..." She traces the pattern in my sweater with the tip of a finger. "It is *not* a 'win-win' for you, is it?"

"That's not for you to worry about."

Tighter nose crunch. "To be plain about it, Cassian, that is bullshit."

I struggle not to laugh. "Is that so?"

"I have a *mind*," she asserts. "And two ears that work."

"I never doubted either, favori."

"I know what Father's voice sounds like, when he is trying to justify a business choice to a colleague. Yours sounded the same way during several calls on your cell phone today. You have walked out in a tree because of this."

"Walked out in a—?" Deep frown. "Do you mean...gone out on a limb?"

She huffs. Waves an impatient hand. "You have taken a risk. A huge one." Her hand slides up, sneaking a little beneath my sweater and caressing the side of my neck. Once more, the breath I've just regulated is a wind storm in my chest. Outwardly, I suck it in as calmly as I can...praying to God the tempest between my legs is equally obedient. "I want to be worth that risk for you, Cassian."

I swallow hard. Run a hand along the back of her arm, up to her neck, around to her nape. "You already are."

"Bullsh—"

I kiss her into silence but with lingering tenderness. "Ssshhh. We're not even halfway through the flight." She draws breath to speak, but I yank it right back out of her with another kiss—still lingering, not as patient. "We have time," I grate. "Lots of time, all right? Let's just—"

And suddenly, I'm the one being cut off with a kiss. Correction: *a kiss*, borrowing my idea but very little else; incinerating my temperance on the sacrificial pyre of her passion. Correction: *her passion*. She is a fireball in my arms: a groaning, grabbing, greedy burst of need, twisting her slender fingers into my hair until our mouths are meshed, our chests are fitted, and our crotches are grinding with inescapable heat...and lust.

Annnnd the discreet hard-on is officially in my rearview. Who the hell have I tried to fool about that, anyway? Discretion is my Dulcinea when she's near. A glorious, impossible dream.

A soundtrack for another time—definitely not when my balls pulse like this, rocketing my shaft to a solid ten on the pain scale. The fucker fills and lengthens, punching at my fly in response to her incredible little mewls and erotic little writhes. *She is going to kill me*, and right now, I can think of no better way to go.

When she finally relents, we are both breathing like goddamn freight trains—but she barely waits before pulling my hand free from her nape and then guiding it down, down, down, until it's formed to her inner thigh. With our gazes still bound, she rolls her hips...sliding her soft flesh against my trembling touch.

But that's not my undoing.

Her awkward little swallow. The tentative flick of her tongue along the seam of her lips. The questioning glint in her eyes, so unsure about what she is doing but trusting herself— trusting *me*—enough to follow the instinct of her desire and do it anyway...

"Wh-What if...I do not want to waste any more time?"

Now I kiss my restraint goodbye.

With a long, slow growl, I dip my head back down while inching my fingertips up. There's a method to the madness— and with her, it *feels* like madness—of being able to read her better through her lips. Their stillness or hesitation will tell me that despite what her brain dictates about honoring my "risk," her body is on an entirely separate page.

So far, we are very much on the same page.

Holy *fuck*, what a page.

As I sweep deeper into the heat of her mouth, my hand explores the silken valley between her thighs. Her skin is soft and shivery beneath my fingertips; her muscles bunch as she undulates in ready response. Pain pricks my scalp as she clings to me tighter, tighter still. "Yes," I hiss, blowing the sound along her lips. "God, yes. Make me feel it, woman. Every shred of it."

She moans and shakes...as I trail my touch higher.

Every. Fucking. Shred.

She arches up. Strangled sounds vibrate in her throat. I kiss down that strained column, reveling in her tension. She's a drawn bow, coiling deeper as I glide a path toward the erotic triangle at her apex. It's shielded by modest panties. I palm her mound through them, my lips hitching as she gasps.

"C-Cassian!"

I growl again. Rub fingers along the fabric's center panel. "Wet panties, sweet Ella. They feel so fucking good."

"Mmmm," she stutters. "I—I am glad you—*ahhhh*." She jerks upward as I circle my fingers. I can feel her clit even through the barrier, trembling...hardening.

"Tell me they're white."

She shoots a confused stare. "Wh-What?"

"Your panties," I clarify. "So help me God, if we were in this airplane alone, I'd be hiking up your skirt to look for myself, but for now, you'll have to let my imagination do the work." I let my gaze grow heavy hoods while running fingers along the inner seams, never delighting in teasing a woman more. She's slick with perspiration and arousal. She smells like tropical flowers and honey.

The crown of my cock is wet now too.

"Color," I manage to command again. "Tell me the fucking color, Mishella."

She gulps again. "Wh-White."

I hiss, exposing my bliss. *Knew it.*

"*Ohhhh.*" It's the only option of a response I give her, working my fingers inward, against her bare flesh. "By the *Creator.* That is...that is so..."

I watch it all take over her face—the wonder, the awe, the heat, the passion—in a transfixed state of my own. Though my cock throbs, damn near screaming for emancipation, it isn't as important as the horizon to which I'm guiding *her.* "Yeah. It is, isn't it?"

"Cassian." She sighs. "Oh...my..."

"My gorgeous girl." I swipe my thumb in, testing the taut bundle at her very center. She jolts and then mewls, fisting my sweater. "You're a virgin to this too, aren't you? Nobody has ever touched you like this before...right here?"

"Oh!" Her head snaps back. "Oh, by all the powers!"

"Tell me, favori. Has anyone—any man—ever stroked you here? Made you this wet and hot?"

"N-No," she finally blurts. "Nobody, Cassian. Only you have touched me like this."

I kiss her softly, conveying my approval. "Now tell me... the naughty way. Tell me how you like my fingers in your pussy. How your wet, succulent clit likes my strokes. How you want me to play with the edges of your tight, virginal tunnel...like this."

"Yes!" It is more rasp than exclamation, though I'm still grateful Doyle has the bedroom door closed. But another part of me mourns the fact, wishing the ass could hear every note of her gasping arousal...wondering if he'd glare at me *now* for the crazy contract commitment. "I—I like your fingers there. Want you...stroking me...touching my clit..."

"And playing with your entrance?"

"And—and playing with my entrance."

"With my cock getting harder, as I think of fucking you there? *Ella?*" I charge it when her lips go still. She's back to remembering the white panties instead of the gorgeous vixen beneath them. But finally she pulls in a harsh breath, squeezes her eyes shut, and forces the obedient words out.

"Yes," she blurts. "Yes—all right—I like it when you think a-about f-fucking me." She breaks in on herself with a moan that has to be the most erotic sound I've ever heard. Curls my sweater tighter in her grip, using the hold as leverage for her whole body, shoving herself against my fingers. It's completely unnecessary. Her fever has infected me too. I flick her erect pearl as fast as I can, snarling in satisfaction when her eyes reopen and her mouth drops in arousal.

"Oh, I'm thinking of fucking you, Ella. Be sure of it." I thrust up my hips until the swells of her ass embrace the head of my cock, and we groan together from the torturous friction. My boxers are soaked, a cruel reminder of how badly I want to be pumping like a heathen inside her tight core. "Hard and hot and deep. You'd be feeling me in your eye sockets. Screaming for me. Pleading to let you c—"

She lurches her head up to deliver the kiss—or maybe yanks mine down, as if it matters—joining our mouths as our bodies crave, an unthinking collision of fire and fervor and flesh as she writhes toward a climax that has me breathing just as hard...needing just as much.

"Let me come, Cassian. Oh, by the sweet fucking Creator, make me come now!"

CHAPTER SIX

MISHELLA

This is not me.

It cannot be.

These are not my words. Not my lips, rambling with these filthy, wanton things; certainly not my body, pulsing with desire I never dreamed possible...heat I never knew existed...

It is all so good.

Too good.

Not me. Not me. Not me.

Not true.

For as Cassian swirls his thumb in and then presses it *there*, punching the hot bundle at my core, I slam back into myself like a soul returned from the dead. I know all of myself, suddenly seeing the past and the present and even the future, for time ceases to exist or matter. Only sensation does, pure and perfect. As my sex screams with ecstasy, my blood is made of stars. My vision is made of light.

My spirit is flown to completion.

"Fuck! Yesssss!"

I ride wave after wave of the silver-white miracle, now unable to utter a sound. Cassian carries me through with words in a baritone gone husky, keeping me from drowning with his strength and his touch. He is my rock...my haven...my all.

The thought is like an icy tide.

Too soon. It is much too soon.

And yet, I cannot deny it.

He bought me. For the next six months, everything I am is his.

Yet every new moment with him brings me closer to...

me.

Whoever that is.

Do I even know? Do I even want to? Will she be a woman I find, only to be forced to hide upon returning to Arcadia? Not being bound to an arranged marriage does not excuse the rest of Father and Mother's proprieties...the remaining walls of their boxes.

Even more terrifying: what if she is a person I do *not* like?

Questions that must remain secrets. I ensure that by dragging my eyes shut as I lift my head, a rag doll in reverse—appropriate, since my body is now limp as one. Cassian assists the feeling by gently massaging my thigh while pulling out from beneath my skirt. His other hand duplicates the pressure along my shoulders. Soon, my head droops to his chest, my senses tempted back toward subconsciousness. I fight them, despite his disciplining growl.

"*Sleep*, Ella. You need it, favori."

"Mmmm. Noooo." I sound slurry and silly, the rag doll animated...sort of. "You," I insist. "I need to...take care of...*you*." Despite the lethargy, I am all too aware that *his* body is still the stiff opposite of mine—especially the part nestled right against my backside. And yes, even in my partial coma, I am aware of how deliciously good it feels.

"I'll be fine."

"That is why you sound like a jungle snake is strangling you?"

He grunts. "Why don't you let *me* worry about the snakes?"

I trump his sound with a giggle. "Or maybe *one* snake?"

His laugh rumbles beneath my ear. "Dirty girl. Are you trying to corrupt me?"

"Hmmphh? No...*no* corruption. *Education.*"

"Ohhhh. Hmmm. Right. *Education.* I can...understand that."

"Have to know the differences between snakes, Cassian." I nestle a little deeper against him. As a yawn takes over, so does a distant memory. Maybe not *so* distant. Was it just yesterday, about this time, that I sat drinking sun tea with Brooke and Vy, being subjected to my own lesson in corruption...and snakes?

"Is that so?" His murmur is warm in my hair. "And what about them?"

"Well, according to Brooke and Vy—"

"But of course..."

"Some are small and harmless," I go on, disregarding his wry tone. "And others are anacondas."

"Huge and dangerous?"

Little frown. "But you are not dangerous."

My dulled logic delays my mortified gasp, though not his chuckle. He tilts up my face, lowering a soft kiss on my nose before murmuring, "*Sleep*, my little *armeau*. You have a bigger adventure ahead than you think. The anaconda agrees with me, whether he likes it or not."

His firm tone demands obedience—and I am too tired to push back anymore. But his sarcasm also dictates a laugh, and on that, I am unable to deliver. *I* am the one choked now—by a thrill that curls down to my toes.

Armeau. He's deliberately labeled me with another

Arcadian word.

It means...

Gift.

CASSIAN

I've lived in New York for nearly ten of my twenty-eight years. Have taken this journey back into the city more times than I can count, gazing at the manmade forest across the Hudson before the Lincoln Tunnel makes the skyline disappear—but over the years have come to think of those buildings as just collections of rooms with collections of people who have nothing but collections of meetings, contracts, conference calls, action plans, presentations, power plans...endless demands of me. Endless lists for me.

The work that rescued me from grief four years ago has become my Manhattan cage.

Until now.

Until, through the eyes of Mishella Santelle, the forest has become magic again. And those eyes, huge as serving platters made from the blue quartz on her island, don't miss a damn thing. Practically bouncing from one side of the limo to the other, scrambling over the bench seat we share to see it all, she is a conduit of enchantment—a sorceress given new powers, courtesy of New York City.

"How do all those buildings *fit*?"

"How many kinds of cars *are* there?"

"What are the yellow ones called?"

"Can we take a ride in one of those big ones with the seats on top?"

"The horns are like music. So pretty."

"Wait. It is...a tunnel...*under the water?*"

"So when the lights turn red, everyone just...*stops?* What if someone does not agree to that?"

"All those people, moving together...they are like pods of dolphins, only on the land..."

She trails into rapt silence after that one. Freezes in place, crouched like an awed kitten over my lap. I rip my gaze away from the perfect curves of her profile, following the line of her stare. It's a quarter to six, so the crowds along 5th are still dominated by business suits and headphones, but she watches the scene as if memorizing every face she sees. I am filled with the same feeling, only my focus frames only one face. I need to remember this moment. *Everything* about it. The azure glitter in her eyes. The twilight breeze in her long curls. The way she's yanked off my blinders and made me see the poetry in New York City crowds.

Don't forget this. Don't forget this.

Especially not now, as she angles her gaze back to me. Blushes a little, as if discerning exactly what I've been up to. "It is incredible, Cassian."

I don't tear my stare from her. "It certainly is, Ella."

She laughs softly and sucks in her bottom lip in that go-to move she has for awkward times. *Little siren;* she doesn't realize that shit makes me yearn to replace her teeth with mine—and use that as only the first place I'll bite her. Maybe one day, I will.

Maybe right *now* I will.

I reach a finger up. Tug at that strawberry-colored pillow, still caught beneath her teeth. Let my gaze dip there, fully informing her of my intention.

I'm going to kiss her. Hard.

"Welcome home, Mr. Court!"

I refrain from lunging out of the car and driving a fist into Scott's cheerful grin. The kid isn't responsible for me losing all track of time and place; I should be grateful he didn't yank open the door and get an eyeful of me lunging down Ella's throat—and maybe up her skirt. *Likely* up her skirt.

I clench my jaw, forcing a smile, before climbing out. "Thanks, Scott. Good to be home."

Things become more fun when his grin turns into curiosity, clearly wondering why I hang on to the back door instead of letting him close it. Scott's love for the Jag XJL is no secret; he exploits every chance to caress his "car baby." Inside five seconds, he's actually a little antsy.

Until I reach back inside and help Mishella step out.

And suppress a chuckle, witnessing the normally smooth college kid become a puddle of astonishment.

If Ella notices the influx of Shar-Pei in his brow, she doesn't show it. Instead, extending a hand with openness and grace, she says, "*Bon sonar.* I...uh...mean, good afternoon. My, what a lovely tie."

Scott runs a hand down the strip of navy-colored satin— and his puffed chest. "Well, thank you." I throw a smug smirk from behind her. If he's not going to mention the tie is part of his required uniform, neither will I.

"Mishella, this is Scott Gaines. He's usually around to drool over the car." I cock a trenchant brow. "And *not* a lot of anything else."

Scott clicks from astonished to stunned. Plenty of women have disembarked from this car before—there's no getting around that, especially with Scott—but to this day, I doubt if the guy knows any of their names. I'm irked with myself about that, until confronted with one irrefutable fact. None of them have stopped to compliment his tie, either.

"So nice to meet you. I am—"

"May I present Mishella Santelle, of the Island of Arcadia." The caveman has stomped in, inspiring my interruption, but I'm not sorry. Handling the introduction allows me to answer the rest of the questions in Scott's gaze. "She'll be staying at Temptation for...a while." Though I am the one who set it, the idea of a time limit on her stay is suddenly repellant—but I accept the twist in my gut. It's likely the first of many to come.

"Oh." At first Scott's response is pleasant. Why wouldn't it be, when basking in the sun of this woman's smile? A second later, my statement sinks in. "*Oh*. Really?"

"Yeah." I arch both brows now. "Really." Translation: *deal with it and behave yourself.*

"Well." The guy bounces on his toes before swooping up Ella's hand and then bowing low over it. "In that case, welcome to Temptation, and consider me at your service."

Mishella laughs. Giggles, really, though she is not a typical giggler. Even that girlish indulgence gets her musical infusion... the kind of harmony that shoots straight to a man's cock as he wonders how to incite it even more. "Merderim. *Bennim honeur*," she murmurs back before translating, "Thank you. It is my honor."

I give Scott two seconds to be charmed by the Arcadian poetry. *One. Two.* Then I step back around, grasping her hand with open possessiveness. "All right, all right. I've got it from here, whelp." Instant gloat, as the melody of a giggle again sprinkles the air—for me.

Scott accepts the trounce with a good-natured bow. "Of course, Mr. Court. I'll take care of the car now."

"I'm sure you will."

I say it while gathering Ella's hand closer. Tucking it under my elbow and resting her elegant fingers along my forearm. It feels so fucking good to have her there. So right. I guide her past the entrance door, set into the brick wall I had installed when renovating this place five years ago. The entrance disguises what lies beyond: a circular forecourt, also made of brick, leading to a marble staircase that swoops up to the mansion's main entrance. Urns with modern lines counteract the gothic impact of it all—and the memories of the woman who loved this place because of that.

Now, for the first time, I see the space through Mishella's marveling gaze. It's new again. Beautiful once more.

My chest rips in conflict.

In remembrance...

I am glad when Mishella stops to peer around more. Use the chance to turn, fisting the center of my sternum. The cavity beneath has been so dark for so long, these new feelings are like a fucking heart attack.

I'm sorry. I'm sorry, *my blossom...*

but maybe it's time for new memories.

"Cassian?"

I spin back around, probably looking as if a ghost has shown up. *And maybe she has.* Lily always did like being the center of attention...

"Hmmm?"

Her eyes find mine—and just like that, my world is filled with nothing else again. The huge blue irises, evoking the sea and skies of her island, bathe me with more warmth and hope and completion than the first time we met. "This...is yours?"

I smile. There's nothing else to do in response to the pure

amazement in her voice. "Yes. It is."

"The whole thing?"

I can't help a soft chuckle. "Well...yes."

"It's like a palais!"

"Not quite."

"It has"—she pauses, her finger in the air, counting the floors—"six levels." Her gaze returns to me, narrowing. "The palace in Sancti has only two more, including the beach and private residence."

I shrug. Instantly recognize the lame excuse of a move—but what other option do I have? "A lot it sits empty." *Fondness for the metaphors today, man?* "I bought it to prove something, at a time in my life when I needed that. But the neighborhood is good, and the views of the Hudson are excellent from the turrets." Not that I'd made the time for reflective moments lately.

"There are *turrets*?" Her head rocks back as she searches the building once more. Watching her like that, hair tumbling down her back, creamy neck exposed, makes me instantly think of her inside one of those towers—hands fogging the windows as I pound into her from behind...

"There are two." I clear the croak from my throat. "They're on the other side."

Her smile lights up her whole face. "Can we go in them?"

"Of course." I add hurriedly, "Well, one." Force a casual shrug. "The other is used for storage. Probably a mess."

A mess. That's a safe way of putting it.

She pops her hands together, enough to serve as proxy for excited applause. "One is just as perfect."

"Then I am at your service." I give Scott's words a deliberately husky inflection. Her smile drops just enough that

I know she's heard...and comprehends.

But first things first.

Introducing her to everyone else.

We cross the ornately tiled vestibule at the top of the stairs and are headed for the waiting elevator when she stops again. Reads the art deco letters etched into the granite over the lift doors.

"Temptation." Her forehead purses. "The building is... actually called that?"

I nod. "It was built in the early twentieth century, in honor of the original owner's wife, whose name was actually Temperance."

"When did irony rear its funny head?"

"Nineteen thirty-three, when the government repealed the Prohibition Act. As soon as that happened, the *new* owners had the first three floors turned into a multi-level supper club. They'd already been operating the basement as a speakeasy for years."

Her frown deepens. "Why would people go to a place just to speak easier?"

"They do it all the time, favori. It's called therapy." When my joke doesn't register, I simply go on, "It's a slang phrase, once used to describe an illegal tavern."

"Illegal?" she retorts. "Why?"

"They just were. As a whole, selling and consuming alcohol was—for many years. Many people thought the stuff was evil."

"But declaring something outside the law...does that not just make it more enticing?"

Fucking great. She has to go and issue one of her little insights now, in that insanely sexy accent, as the lift doors close and we're sealed in for half a minute.

Half a minute is all I need.

I sweep around, pinning her against the elevator's cage, before dipping and taking her lips beneath mine. I'm not savage about the move, though I yearn to be. The contrast of her soft curves against the ornate steel...and thinking of taking her hard enough to embed the pattern into her flesh...

Fuck. *Fuck.*

What is this woman doing to me?

I pull away enough to stare into her impossibly gorgeous eyes. In the dimness of the lift, they've turned the color of smoke. "For the record," I rasp, "you're forbidden to say 'enticing' again, unless we're alone."

A slow smile teases at her lips. "And if I do not heed your... decree?"

I dip my head in a mock threat. "Punishment. Merciless. For certain."

"I shall make a note of that."

"In what journal would that go in?"

"Oh, I think a new one shall have to be created." Her fingers toy at my sweater. Her smile flirts with my gaze. "'Cassian's Disciplines?'"

"God*damn.*" I push closer, letting *her* crotch feel what that does to *mine.* "That has a very nice ring to it..."

I'm inches away from smashing another kiss on her, devil take the consequences, when the lift *thunk*s to a stop at level six—and surprise, surprise—Lucifer himself is waiting with a glare for us, right through the steel mesh. All right, so Hodge is a close enough comparison, and that's before Prim arrives on the scene. She has to be near; obviously Scott called upstairs the second Ella and I left his sight.

Sure enough, as soon as the door opens and I help Mishella onto the landing, Prim rounds the corner from the kitchen. Her blonde dreadlocks are twisted into a high bun, making it even easier to note the fiery shade of her gold eyes. Fury will do that to a woman—especially this one.

Despite Prim's ire spiking the air, Mishella slips her hand free from mine and then reaches out, as amiable as she was with Scott. "Hello. It is good to meet you. My name is Mishella. And yours?"

Prim glares as if Ella's fingers are scorpions—until her eyes snatch up to meet mine, as I have known they would. I return the scrutiny with a sole, silent message. *Play nice. We'll talk later.*

Her pierced nose flares a little. *You bet your ass we will.* She makes short work of accepting the handshake and then stating, "Prim Smith. And before you ask, it's not short for anything. And before you start laughing, I like my name fine."

"Why would I laugh?" Ella's nose crinkles. "I like it too. It is unique. And pretty."

"Thank you."

There's civility in it. Just a toss. I still grab it for the win. My little sorceress has melted *Prim* after just thirty seconds. *Alert the press.*

While the advent is significant, it confuses the hell out of Hodge. My burly curmudgeon of a houseman collects his paychecks from me but signed his heart away to Prim at least a year ago—not that she'll ever notice. Still, Prim's not jabbed the expected iceberg into Ella's *Titanic*, clearly causing his internal debate. "So...uh...Boss, are there bags to handle? I think Scott said some are coming up on the service elevator?"

Ah. Conflict handled with the man's default to practical

hospitality. I accept *it* for the win too. "He's correct. Just put them in the master bedroom."

"Sure thing, Boss."

"The master bedroom?"

I ignore Prim's snip, turning Ella's attention toward Hodge. "This is Conchobhar Hodgkins, houseman and engineer extraordinaire—but we call him Hodge for obvious reasons. He'll be your call for anything from heavy lifting to rewiring the lights."

"And an occasional green smoothie." Hodge jams hands into his back pockets and nervously toes the floor. He's not used to bantering socially but is clearly falling under Ella's spell as quickly as Scott did—though has held out twice as long as *I* was able.

"Oh." Her smile widens. "That sounds delicious."

"If one enjoys drinking the lawn for lunch," Prim mutters.

Mishella laughs but kills the sound off when struck by Prim's cold fish of an attitude. I'm tempted to locate my own inner mackerel and show Prim what a real seafood smackdown is like but am thawed once more by the hand curled beneath my elbow and the eager smile beaming past my shoulder. In this moment, I'm certain the woman can probably talk me out of a kidney. Probably both. Suddenly, the wars fought over Helen of Troy and Ann Boleyn don't seem so idiotic.

"So do I get my tour now?"

I tuck her hand in tighter. Return her grin like a goofy fool—and perhaps I *am* one. At least she's not asking for a war—or a kidney. "You bet."

"Even the turret?"

"The turret!"

Prim's outcry turns me back around—along with the look

I've been rehearsing for her since the takeoff from Arcadia. Because I knew this moment would arrive. That there'd be *one* chance to communicate this message in the space of a stare.

Mishella Santelle is staying for six months, whether you're happy about it or not. Which means we're cooling it about Turret Two, also whether you like it or not.

Prim's nostrils flare again. Her lips jam into a line of resignation. I nod and declare to Mishella, "We can *start* with the turret, if you like."

She really indulges a laugh now. "Let us begin with wherever *you* like. I want to see it all, so it does not matter."

As I guide her toward the main living room, it's not without a parting stare from Prim—and the knowing truth attached in those deep amber irises. And the sadness layered beneath that.

She wants to see it all, hmmm? Well, good luck with figuring that *one out, Cas.*

But Prim knows the answer to *that* already too.

There will be no "figuring that one out."

Because in the end, even Mishella Santelle doesn't get to see it all. Not every corner of my home...*not* every room in my heart...and *not* the fucking ghost who lives in both.

Not the parts of me that are best left in that grave with her.

It makes sense now: the decision I made back on Arcadia, to call this thing at six months. It's enough time to savor the heaven...without fearing the hell will rise up. Because, as I already know all too clearly, hell has a way of doing that. But for six months, I can bribe away the demons. After that, they can have my soul again. I'm sure the damn thing will never be the same after this, anyway.

CHAPTER SEVEN

MISHELLA

Curious.

Even thousands of miles from home, midnight feels exactly the same.

The sounds are different: a wilderness bustling with cars and trains and people instead of wind and waves and birds. The smells are different too: steam and steel and the foods of a thousand cultures, instead of the island aroma that has always brought reminders of only one thing: the water. This is *not* a complaint. I love the sea; it is the Creator's perpetual gift to Arcadia—but it has always, simply, been there. Then again the next day. And the next. And the next.

This island...is a new world every other minute, even at midnight. Beyond the turret's windows, I watch it all: the people bustling, the horns honking, the trains whooshing, the sirens screaming. The chaos seems to mesh, becoming a peace of its own. A manmade ocean.

It is the respite I need.

The synergy giving me shelter from thoughts that will not stop taunting.

From the memories...

Of that conversation.

The one I was not supposed to overhear. Cassian and Prim,

hiding themselves in the pantry off the kitchen after dinner, clearly thinking I was still enraptured by all the technical doo-dads of the living room. Granted, the temptation was certainly there—so many wonderments to play with, hidden cleverly by the wood, glass, and leather décor—but manners are always more important than amusement, so I got up to help clear the table.

Only to wish I had not.

"What the hell *were you thinking, Cassian?"*

"Prim—"

"Wait. Wrong question. You're always thinking. Just which head was it with this time?"

"Goddammit. This is about more than that."

"And you don't think I'm afraid of that too?"

"Now *what are* you *about?"*

"Oh God, Cas. Have you thrown up the blinders that high— or do you see it and just choose to ignore it?"

"I'm not 'ignoring' a fucking thing!"

"Of course not. Which is why you flew that girl home from the middle of the Mediterranean and then moved her right into the master with you. Let me guess. She was wasting away in the cinders somewhere, and Prince Charming had to ride in with the magic slipper. Wait; no. Perhaps she was a wilting flower, ready to bloom. Eliza Doolittle, filthy island style. Enter Professor fucking Higgins, ready to make that rain in Spain fall mainly on the plain."

"Yeah. Right. That's *it exactly."*

"Are...are you laughing *about this? Why the hell are you laughing?"*

"Because you're not making any sense."

"I'm making perfect sense. Dear God, more sense than I

want to make. She doesn't just punch one button for you, does she? She punches both. *That's why you didn't come home with just the T-shirt."*

"The...what?"

"You went to the island. Banged the local wahine. *You should've come home with the damn T-shirt. Instead, you came home with the girl.* God. *You are such a moron."*

"Dammit, Prim. Keep it down. And for the record, I didn't bang her."

"You mean you haven't yet. I'll take that lovely silence as a yes. *And after you do, what do you think will happen? That she'll happily hop on a plane back home, without asking for a* cent *in 'compensation for services rendered?'"*

"It's not like that, either."

"So you are *compensating her?"*

"All right. This conversation is over."

I did not linger to confirm if it really was or not. Had the damage not already been done? That answer vibrates throughout the clamp remaining on my chest—that has been there ever since making my excuses from staying for Prim's "famous tiramisu" to retire early, feigning exhaustion from our traveling.

At least it bought me time to prepare for bed—in all the awkward senses of the word—for my first night in a man's bed. It did *not* halt my mind from racing with every possible, horrible, incredible scenario that might come. Would he seduce me gently? Taunt me with another version of what he did to me on the plane? Or simply launch into bed and fuck me wildly?

Oh. Yes. *Option number three...please?*

A brutal breath sucks through my lips. A flush invades my

neck and breasts. Heat surges between my thighs. Even my mouth aches, craving the dominance of his once more...as it has since the moment that he finally did come to bed...

Then, after but a few minutes, fell into a drained slumber.

After that, as Brooke would say, my choice of action was a no-brainer. The second his breaths evened into deep sleep, I was out of bed, into my slippers, and headed for this exact spot. The turret is my favorite part of his tour from earlier, perhaps because he's restored it to its art deco grandeur rather than installing the high-gloss look prevailing over the rest of the building's interior. Granted, the first three floors of the place are satellite offices for Court Corporation, modern by necessity—but the other areas feel "off" to me, as if the design is a deliberate attempt to shut out the past.

More disturbingly, especially after my accidental eavesdrop on Cassian and Prim's argument, I sense there is actually a past to shut out.

The recognition brings a heavy sigh.

"I'd offer a penny for those thoughts, but it sounds like they're worth a dollar."

The commentary from a few feet back, roughened by recent sleep, is a surprise because it is *not* a surprise. The air I breathe in for the sigh is the same air that shifts, making room for his presence. Just like it did in the palais back on Arcadia... and has ever since.

Only all those times, I was not trying to inhale around a vise in my chest.

I do not turn, not wanting Cassian to see my grimace. *Idiot.* Why should he *not* see it...and know the conflict weighing on me? Prim made no secret of hers.

"I...could not sleep. Time difference, I suppose." *Or the*

hundred ways I keep wondering why Prim's input is such a priority to you.

"Is that all? Just the jet lag?" He stretches on the floor next to me, leaning on an elbow as opposed to my stomach-down recline. The reading chaise behind us is comfortable enough, but being closer to the city's energy is a better fit for my spirit tonight. He sees that too. I discern it in the forests of his eyes.

Does he see the rest of my thoughts?

His query has not made that clear. I worry that he does... and that he does not.

"You must be just as thrown out of your kilt as me," I finally offer—to be met by a chuckle that should not be as sexy as it is.

"Off-kilter?" he offers. "Though I'm not opposed to kilts *or* taking them off, if that's the request." He sobers a little while tugging at his hair, which tumbles lushly into his eyes. "Scottish is somewhere in my mutt mix, which is why my hair turns a little red in the sun...or so Mom tells me."

"Your maimanne?" This new revelation tempers my jealousy about Prim—for the moment. "Are you two close?"

A smile remains on his face but changes. Softens. "Yeah. You could say that."

"Why?" I return. "Why...could I say that?"

His smile evaporates. "We've been through a lot together. *A lot.*" His shoulders stiffen. "Perhaps it's best we leave it there."

"Of course." I swivel my head, resting it atop my hands, again attempting to put aside the petty hurt in my heart. "You have others to confide in, after all."

So much for attempting—or even kidding myself that I

did. But the dig is vague. He has as much right to toss it aside as I did to make it. If he does, then at least I know exactly where I stand. If he does not...

He definitely does not.

Bracing a hand around the back of my neck, he jerks my stare back up to him. The gesture is an unsettling mix of command and calm—reminding me all too clearly of how he took over things in my bedroom, back on Arcadia. Was that just two nights ago? Only a heartbeat has passed since then, right?

No.

A forever has passed.

"You heard," he grates. "Didn't you? Prim and me. In the pantry." He shakes his head. Gets down a leaden swallow. "Never mind. I know you did. I felt you there. Standing at the sink."

Forget about unsettled. I am suddenly frightened—gripped by spectral shivers, such as the ones I have known while working late in the palais and glimpsing the building's famous ghosts in my periphery. Only now, the otherworld does not hide in the shadows. It is here, in the air between us...in the dazzle of emeralds in Cassian's eyes, in the promise of fire in his touch...in the confirmation that he knows me, senses me, feels me just as I do him.

In the magic of us.

"Prim is a good friend, Ella. Nothing more."

But you have history with her. A lot of it.

I cannot bring myself to utter it. "She has the right to feel... what she feels."

He grunts. Retorts through his teeth, "The fuck she does."

"She cares about you. It is a glaring truth, Cassian, from

the first second she gazes upon you." I curl a hand against his cheek, as if I can actually soothe his ire. "I do not blame her."

He presses his hand over mine. Runs it down to my elbow with nearly punishing pressure. "I don't want to talk about her right now."

"But..."

"But what?"

I push to a sitting position. Pull my arm down—as far as he will let me. His hold on my elbow remains firm and determined. "*Am* I just a 'rescue project' to you, Cassian? The Eliza Doolittle you yanked from the slums, and—"

He shoves to his feet. I almost expect him to punch one of the walls or windows, but he becomes scarier, not moving, his posture impossibly erect. "Is that what you believe?" Every word is so low, they are almost drowned by a pair of emergency sirens down on the street, their wails growing.

"I...I do not want to."

I let my head fall, but that brings even more bizarre sensations. Sitting here, my gaze filled with his bare feet, I feel...intimate with him. Stripped for him.

Connecting...

I lean forward. Just enough to touch his knee with my forehead. He's only wearing white cotton pants, and I realize he must have yanked them out of his luggage. They smell the way he did on Arcadia: his cedar and soap blended with ocean wind and oranges...

And there's something else now. A smell unique to New York. Musky. Masculine. *Really* erotic.

Before I can breathe it in again, he is next to me. *Next* to me, plummeted back to the floor. Both his hands dig into my hair, forcing my gaze up into his.

Connecting...

"Don't you see?" he rasps into the inches between our lips. "*Can't* you see?" And then his mouth is on me, molding me... needing me. Then rasping, "Mishella. My favori. My perfect armeau. I brought you here because I'm a selfish bastard who hasn't had anyone like you in my world in..." He stops, shaking his head, gaze glittering once more, a thousand shades of confusion. "In a very long time.

"Mishella Santelle...it is *you* who have rescued *me*."

CASSIAN

What the fuck have you done?

My head machetes me with the words. My gut gladly joins in.

But my heart and my soul have never felt more perfect. Yeah...for the first time in my life, perfect and petrified are happy pals, powering their way into the arms that crush around her, the body that fits against hers...

The cock that swells between us.

"*Cassian.*" Her whisper is high and ragged, verbally interpreting the tears that hovers so beautifully in her eyes. I gaze hard into their glimmer, willing the wetness to break free. To cleanse me, rescue me all over again. To grant me permission for what I've been craving since the moment my skin first touched hers, during that formal reception back on Arcadia. She knows it too. I see it in the quiver of her lips, in the choppy pulse in her neck, in the little trembles of her fingers, all ten raising up, bracing my jaw.

Finally, they thicken, brim...and escape.

My perfect invitation.

I crash my mouth back down.

Invade hers without hesitation. Claim her without compunction. Kiss her like she's my last fucking breath.

As our mouths continue to chase and tease and caress and conquer, our bodies slide all the way to the floor. When we break apart for air, I drag my gaze open to feast again on the sight of her, now awash in the glow of the streetlights and the moon. She's wearing a light-blue sleep set tonight, coaxing out dazzling sparks of silver in the stare she returns to me. *My beautiful gift.*

I dip in, kissing her once more. With reverence this time. With thanks.

When her fingers caress down to my chest, I don't feel so reverent anymore. *Keep it together. Keep. It. Together.*

The mantra pounds my blood, even as my dick throbs against her hip. Harder still as she glides her touch across me, a look of wonder in those blue-silver irises. My nipples stiffen for her. My abs tauten, cinching in my breath.

*Go lower. Oh fuck...*don't *go lower.*

I seize my sole moment of self-control, grab her wrist, and slowly lower it to the floor on her other side. With our stares still latched, I rasp, "You know what they say about turnabout..." Actually, I'm *not* sure if she knows—but the anticipation of what she'll transform it into already enchants my mind and takes my cock along for the ride.

"Mmmm." She lifts a modestly flirty look—quite possibly the only woman on the planet who *can*. "That *is* one I know."

Her start-and-stop sigh finishes it—as I yank on the ribbon enclosure of her top, baring her breasts to my view.

And what a fucking view.

She's more exquisite than I imagined. Round, firm, and

full, with flesh a shade paler than the parts of her that get year-round Arcadian sun...a perfect contrast to the sweet strawberries of her nipples, jutting from dusky, tight areolas. They pucker right before I lean in, worshiping her with soft nips and licks, until she's writhing beneath me...

And then I use my teeth.

"Oh! By the powers! *Cassian*."

I palm the breast I'm attending. Constrict it a little, forcing more blood into her throbbing tip, before I bite again. As she screams, I suckle away the pain. When I shift to her opposite peak, she mutters something in Arcadian and drives her hand through my hair, forcing my mouth down harder.

It drives me crazy. In all the good ways.

Too many ways.

I reach up, snaring her hand again. Swing it over her head until it's pinned to the floor there. In the same violent sweep, I thoroughly embed my thighs against hers. Push up, notching the bastard of a ridge in my pants against the sweet, wet patch in hers, until we're dry-humping like kids stealing a quickie between classes, fast and fierce and feverish.

"Fuck. Me."

"Take. Me."

"You're so...*hot*."

"You are so...*huge*."

"I...we...have to...slow down."

"Wh-What? *Why?*"

"Can't...hold back. Not for much...longer."

"Then do not. For Creator's sake, Cassian, *please!*"

I rear up. Try to shake my head. That's a big fucking *try*. "No. There's no do-over on this. I'm going to make this good for you, dammit." In my head, I already have a vision of how this should go. Candlelit bath, champagne by the fire, and *then* the roll in the sheets, going as gently as I can. Nothing in there about screwing her senseless in the turret, in the middle of the night, with half of Manhattan watching. Okay, Manhattan probably doesn't care, but that's beside the point. "It's going to be the best for you. It's going to be—"

Her laugh cuts me short, so manic it's cute. "Cassian, if it is more 'the best' than this, you will kill me from sheer pleasure."

I let a taut growl go free. "With all due respect, favori, let *me* worry about your death-by-pleasure."

Her nose crinkles. It disappears into a stare of pure resolve—an unnerving sight, for the second I'm still able to think—before her hand is under my pants and all over my erection, milking the precome I've somehow kept at bay. Not anymore. I turn into one groan after the next as the drops escape, searing and perfect—and torturous. With every one of my moans, her smile kicks up a little higher, until I'm not sure what's snipping the neurons in my brain quicker: her perfect touch or her incredible beauty.

"Stop!" I finally groan it out. "For the love of Christ, Ella, stop or I'll come all over your hand."

Her eyes darken. Her teeth catch her bottom lip. "And how would that not be 'the best,' either?"

My growl lengthens. Little minx, goading me on to more. Notation for my own journal: my proper little Arcadian likes filthy verbal foreplay.

A detail that deserves a little more...testing.

With a commanding yank, I tug her hand back out. With a brutal sweep, slam it again to the floor. Our bodies slide back together, hard to soft, pulse to pulse, arousal to arousal. Her chest surges up, stabbing her nipples against mine. Her mouth falls open on another gasp, nearly begging for my kiss.

I don't give it to her.

Instead, I linger inches above her, savoring the taste of her anticipation, giving her something even better. The words. "Do you like this, favori? Do you like being flattened on the floor beneath me, trembling and aching for me? Do you like my erect cock against you, leaking come in its need for you?"

"Oh," she grates. "Oh...yes."

"*Oh yes* is fucking right." I dip my lips to her neck. "I can feel it in your pulse, Ella. Taste it on your skin. And I treasure it...everywhere."

I emphasize that with another roll of my hips. Rejoice in the answering buck of hers, adorable little jerks responding to nothing but her most primitive instincts. Have I ever been with a woman like her, so open to feeling everything and thinking about nothing? Have I ever *known* anyone like her, so transparent about her desire, uncaring that her hair isn't "fanned out" just so, that her feet aren't "daintily pointed," that the sounds bursting from her throat are awkward and rough instead of a mewling porn kitten?

She is a revelation.

A sensual, incredible burst into my psyche. Into my world.

My logic defaults to the only possibility. My lips burst with it while continuing to suckle her delicious skin. "*Sorceress.* Dear fuck...that has to be it. You're a sorceress, woman, and I've become your willing slave." I lock her other wrist down with my grip. Rise up, deliberately exposing my muscles and might against her silken skin and curves. "Look at this. Look at *you*. Do you know what power you have over me, even in your shackles? How your beauty—" I stop, needing to fit breath around the space now occupied by her. "You command me,

Mishella. God*damn*...you possess me."

Her own chest pumps, matching the desperate cadence of mine. "*Cassian.*"

I shake my head again. My hair falls into my eyes, but I drill a solid stare through the mess at her. "Look at you... begging me. But *I'm* the one who should be pleading with *you.*"

"Oh...no. Oh...*yes*..."

"You rule me, woman. You...destroy me."

As the confession soughs out, I scrape both thumbs across her pulse points. Slide them up, until they dig into the centers of her palms. Deeper...deeper...

Holy Mary, Mother of God, pray for this sinner...because he wants to sin like he's never sinned before, and the only redemption is *the sin. The only heaven left is her...*

"Tell me." Now I'm the beggar—and it finally feels perfect. "I need to know. I'm your convert. Your slave. What do you bid of me, sorceress...*goddess*...?"

Her fingers curl around mine. Her back arches, her thighs constrict...her pussy softens. "Destroy me too," she whispers. "Cassian, *please*...take me. Fuck me."

My own muscles shake—fighting the surge of heat her plea brings. I breathe raggedly. I've expected the words, so why do they make me feel regressed to sixteen again? Why does air feel like fire as I force it in down my nostrils? Why am I an all-thumbs idiot after rising to pull off her pajama bottoms and then mine?

And now, why does the sight of her mound make my cock drip all over again?

I stare at the rigid fucker, finally admitting my bewilderment. I've always been a Brazilian fan: the football teams, the food, and definitely the bikini wax. But Arcadia is nowhere near Brazil, and the reality here is, again, as I expected—except for one astonishing difference. Beholding Ella's unshaved "wilderness" has turned *up* my desire—especially when the evidence of *her* lust forms glittering beads on her tawny curls.

"Fuck. Me." My snarl only hints at the toll she and her enchantress pussy already take. *Need to...get in there...so bad.*

"A wonderful idea." Her throaty rasp more perfect torture—to which she adds a *coup de grace*, kneading her breasts until the tips are stiff and red. "Cassian. By the Creator—I need you *now.*"

My dick throbs against my palm. *Hell yes*, it screams—

To be countermanded by my brain. And its evil sense of humor.

Evil.

"You need me, hmmm?" I line myself up, pointing my glistening crest toward her exquisite entrance. "This, right here? You need...this?"

Her whole body tremors. Her hands work her flesh harder. "Yes," she pants. "Oh *yes*!"

"Not yet." I chuckle in answer to her moan of despair. "First, not without this." Thank fuck I remember Doyle's stash of condoms in the table next to the chaise. This is probably the first time I'm thankful for being aware of the "accessories" he likes to leave behind all over the house. "And second," I continue while sheathing up, "not without you showing me more of...this."

My free hand illustrates the point, running through the slickness between her thighs. Though it elicits a higher cry, she manages to stammer, "Th-This? Wh-What...do you...mean?"

"I mean show it to me, Ella. With both hands. Take them

off your tits. Slide them into your pussy. Rub them on your lips and then spread yourself with them. Let me see the gorgeous cunt I'm going to fuck."

Without another question, she obeys. Dear God, so perfectly...proving I was wise to make that mental journal entry in ink. This woman, and her gorgeous passion, thrive on nasty words like a flower in the sun. As she blooms for me, I grow for her, my flesh filling the rubber...straining for the slick, tight tunnel beyond her dripping curls.

The depths I'll mark for the first time.

The place I'll have in her soul...forever.

The virginity I'll claim...and cherish.

"*Damn*." Great. *That's* eloquent. But nothing else is possible in the moment I fit myself to her opening and push into the impossible softness...the resistant walls.

I halt when she winces. "It—it is all right," she protests. "I—I am all right. Probably just a little..." A sheepish shrug, a stunning blush. "Scared."

I dip my head, kissing her. "It's all right to be scared. But it's also all right to breathe, favori."

She laughs. For a moment. "Oh. Yes. *That*."

I take advantage of her distraction to push deeper. Clench back a groan, letting that privilege belong to her. "Good, Ella. You're doing good, my little beauty." Brilliance strikes. "Try to bear down a little. Just pretend it's a couple of your fingers, only fuller."

"My—my *fingers*?"

Okay. Screw the brilliance. "Fuck," I mutter, punctuating with another laugh. "Well, that explains things a little."

"A little...like what?"

"Like why you're so goddamn tight...and good." I've used

the conversation for the same nefarious purpose: now, I'm nearly two-thirds in.

And blindingly ready to give her the rest.

"So."

A small test thrust.

"Fucking."

A deeper one.

"*Good.*"

She doesn't scream.

She *does* try to tear off a layer of my back flesh as her body accepts the last inch of mine. My mouth opens, needing to tell her to relax, but I selfishly savor one more second of her tension and what it does to the suction power of her walls.

Pray for us sinners...

Now, and at the hour of our death...

Yeah. That's it. That *has* to be. I've died, and this is heaven, and—

She really has destroyed me.

"*Ella.*" There's nothing left on my lips but her name. Nothing left in my senses but *her*, surrounding me, consuming me—propelling me to an ether comprised solely of that place in space and time where our bodies pulse together, our hearts hammer together. "*Mishella,*" I whisper this time, squeezing the globes of her ass, forcing her tighter around me. "We're there. You're there. Feel me, favori. Feel all of me..."

"Mmmm." It's not a pleasant hum. It's the *I'm trying* sound, and I don't fucking like it. But the moment I withdraw even a millimeter, she scratches once again. The sorceress has claws. Sharp ones.

She pulls her arms in, shifting her hold to my jaw. Forces my lips to hers in a kiss that's so searing, it's haunting. As our mouths mesh and our tongues swirl, I am suddenly able to feel her soul, to see inside her heart...for they are the same as mine. *Remember. This.* The tastes of it, passion and salt and need. The smells of it, sex and skin and jasmine. The sounds of it, roaring in my ears and throbbing through my blood. The feeling of it, a magic that will follow me until those suspended moments between life and death, when all the best moments of my life return...and I pray more of them await me on the other side.

Unless that moment is now.

As she begins to rock her hips, working her body around mine.

As she arches her head back, releasing a sibilant sorceress sigh.

As she cries out, in the second I slide my touch between our bodies, to finish her first.

And she dies too...convulsing through the most perfect end I've ever witnessed. The orgasm strains her muscles, bulges her eyes...and squeezes every inch of her pussy.

Dear. Fuck.

Over and over she seizes me, her body signing the death warrant for mine. I am executed in a hot, consuming flood, life pouring from me, immense and primal...

And perfect.

"Do not...stop. Oh please, Cassian. I think I might...oh, *again.* Do not stop!"

"Never." I grate it into her neck while continuing to pump her pussy and work her clit. "Never, sweet armeau."

When I take the throbbing little nub and pinch just the tip, she finally gives me her scream. She vibrates, wild and unthinking, gripping me in desperate need, like the fucking angel leading her to heaven.

She has no idea...of how things really are.

That *she's* the angel. The enchantress gifted from the clouds...to lead me back from hell.

Morose thoughts—for much later. Now, I only want to think about her laugh in my ear, the mix of melody and husk that brings satisfaction as complete as her climaxes, making my resolve official. This really is where I want to die. Right here, right now. Surely, no other moment in my life is going to equal this perfection.

"Oh...my...high...holy...Creator." She lets her arms sprawl, limp as noodles, straight out to her sides. I chuckle my way into a new kiss, letting my grip slide along them, until our fingers are again twined.

"Certainly took the sting out of jet lag."

"Jet lag." She repeats it softly, her face remaining dazed. "So...how long does that last?"

I laugh again, not missing the hopeful lilt with which she finishes. "Not sure."

"Why not?"

"Usually too keyed up to pay attention to it."

"Hmmm."

It's the hum I'm used to—on the other hand, hope to never be used to because it's so damn adorable. Half of it is barely audible, since she's already dedicated half her brain to at least eight layers of deeper thought. The exciting part is watching her cycle through them and wondering what she'll say to make the wait worth it.

"Perhaps we should try to find out."

Definitely worth it.

After grinding a slow, savoring kiss into her, I answer, "Perhaps we fucking *should.*"

CHAPTER EIGHT

MISHELLA

By now, I am fairly certain there is no such thing as a three-day, debilitating case of jet lag—at least not in Cassian Court's world. But right now, it is not a point I care to argue. Or think about. As if I am capable of either, with my gaze consumed by the sight of his dark-gold hair spilling over my lower belly...and the ecstasy of his tongue stabbing into my intimate hole, over and over and over...

My abdomen clenches. My backside pinches in.

Oh, dear Creator...

Close.

A few more. Please...

Close.

I am not even aware of the words spilling off my lips, until his growl interjects—and his head pulls up. "Not yet, armeau. Not...yet."

I whine, protesting and almost angry, reaching back to grab the pillows. There have to be a dozen of them on his big bed, and for a fleeting second, I wonder why I do not know the exact count. I have barely left these sheets for seventy-two hours. Surely there was time to count all his pillows at some point...

But there was not. Not between sleeping and...things like this.

Lots and lots and *lots* of this.

The most perfect three days of my life.

Consumed with giving myself to the most perfect man in the world.

His body like a gold marble god, taut and defined as he rolls on a condom. His face lined with fierce passion as he gazes over my spread nudity. His eyes, shimmering and sharp, as he scrapes fingernails down my thighs, to my knees...

And slams my legs wide.

"Keep them like that," he orders. "The whole time I'm fucking you." A moment later, he prompts, "What do you say to that?"

"Y-Yes, Cassian."

He knows I'll barely get it out. He *knows* what his rougher, filthier side does to me. How all his dirty words affect me, incinerating the bonds of propriety that have been the hallmarks of my existence for so long. With the words, he gives me no choice about leaving them behind...about becoming his perfect little investment.

And I do feel perfect.

Adored.

Desired.

Worthy.

His face tightens as he positions himself at my entrance. His body is hard...everywhere. I raise my arms, anxious to learn its formidable landscape once more, but he growls, "No. Leave them where they are. Grip the pillows. It lifts your luscious tits...so perfectly." He sucks and bites one and then the other, still taunting my entrance with his cock. "You like that, don't you? When I make your nipples erect like this? When you know exactly what it does to my dick?"

I struggle for breath. "Oh...*y-yes*, Cassian."

"And does it make you hot too, little Ella?"

"Yes, Cassian."

"Does it make your tunnel wet? Turn you into my horny, sweet sorceress, ready to be fucked?"

"Yes, Cassian."

He lifts back up. Digs his hands into my hips, pulling my body another inch around his, opening the view to his heated gaze—and mine. The sight of his shaft, absorbed into the softness of my core, is as mesmerizing as the rest of him. Muscles straining. Power coiling. Passion building. He is beautiful, rippled...stunning.

"Then use the words." He intensifies his grip along with the dictate. "Tell me what you want...with the words *I* want."

I swallow hard. There will be no getting away with a gentle morning screw. This explosion is going to be nuclear...for both of us.

"Take me," I rasp. "Please...deep inside...with your cock. Take your payment back from my body until I cannot see straight. Until I scream from being filled by you—"

Then I *do* scream as he plows me hard and hot. No inch of my sex is left wanting. He handles me like a piece of clay, subjected to the pound of his ruthless hammer. In a sense, I am. Less than a week after even meeting the man, I am a being recreated...an artwork unveiled with every slice of his chisel...

Then shattered.

Blown apart into a thousand pieces of being, of feeling, of frantic, perfect fulfillment...

"Take it."

"Yes, Cassian."

"All of my cock."

"Yes, Cassian."

"In your perfect cunt."

"Yes...yes...*yes!*" The pieces of me explode into dust. "Cassian!" I am nothing but sensation, climaxing hard, senses rejoicing as he dissolves with me, coming deep inside me.

And for the fiftieth time in the last week, I wonder if I truly will ever be the same.

Or if I want to be.

Before I can delve into the morose possibilities for answers to that, Cassian's phone vibrates on the nightstand—for the twentieth time this morning. He groans. I giggle.

"I knew I'd regret telling the world I'm back on the grid."

"I think our jerk is up, Mr. Court."

For some reason, that quirks his lips. "Jig."

"Now?" I glance down. At the moment, dancing in any form is rather out of the question.

He explains only by popping a quick kiss to my forehead before reaching for the device with a brisk swipe. "Rob. Good morning."

Between getting his hands on—and in—me, the man has at least divulged that "Rob" is short for Robin, who, in an even more confusing twist, is a young man in his first job out of college. From what I can tell, Rob is succeeding. In the last seventy-two hours, Cassian has entrusted him with everything from changing security passwords—a weekly ritual at Court Enterprises—to things a little more personal, like scheduling a physician appointment for his boss today.

That being known, Cassian still earns a new dose of my amazement with the tone, as if he's standing in a board room instead of prone in bed, still buried inside me. "Better, thanks," he continues. "Scheduling that fast turnaround for the Arcadia trip was probably too aggressive. I'm current on emails and the latest reports though"—he shrugs at my when-did-*that*-happen gawk—"and I'll be coming in today. That face-to-face with Flynn Whelan is too important. Have his people confirmed for lunch? Good. Make sure the catering team brings up that Italian water he likes. Any other notable calls?"

It sounds like Rob hesitates but delivers the reply in a businesslike tone. Cassian matches the timbre—on the surface. Beyond the new shutters over his expression, I see the same discomfort that first stopped Rob—though he quickly cloaks it. I am not sure whether to be relieved or angry. The resulting confusion makes me restless. I shift, pull away, and leave for the bathroom—as if the sliding wood door can keep out the river-stone perfection of his voice, smoothness and power beneath each baritone syllable.

"No. You responded as you should have, Rob. She's been fishing for a definitive on the Literacy Ball for a few months. Jumping up the chain and turning in the RSVP herself... Well, I'll applaud her for the guts, if not the intelligence." Heavy huff, through a definitive pause. "Call Yolanda Wood at the Literacy Guild. Clarify my RSVP *is* for two, but I'll phone myself with my guest's name by EOB today. It will definitely *not* be Amelie Hampton's."

I finish my business, debating whether to follow my original plan and start the shower or find a journal and note the name *Amelie Hampton*. The knot in my belly supports the latter. It is not simply the stress she has brought to Cassian—whoever she is—though that *is* a start. It is the discomfiting questions now raised in my heart—and the anger that rises in their wake.

Did you think he was living a monk's life before you arrived?

Did you think because he moved you into his bedroom, he planned on keeping himself *out of others?*

Did you think he doesn't have a hundred other "Amelie Hamptons" across this city? This country?

I shake my head, forcing the funk away. With a short huff, crank on the shower. Climb in under the wonderfully hot spray, deliberately turning from the granite seat upon which my backside has been planted numerous times over the last few days—for the most erotic of reasons. Right now, it is best to deal strictly with the steam from the water instead of those salacious visions—and how many women from Cassian's past share the exact same memories.

Too late.

As he enters the bathroom, clearly finished with Rob, it is too easy to imagine him walking in on another girl, in another time, and tossing his condom in the trash with the same laser accuracy. It is even more effortless to think of him turning and peering through the stall glass, the same dimpled smirk on his face...with the same dreamy follow-through.

"Why'd you start in there without me?"

Oh, yes. All the others have surely felt just like this as well—body newly tingling, senses freshly awakened, tongue perfectly tied—as he plants those long fingers against his corded hips, purposefully pulling attention to that magnificent appendage at their juncture...

I. Will. Not. Look. I. Will. Not. Look.

I steal a small glance. Just one. *Dear sweet Creator, why did you build him with such magnificence? Especially* there?

I manage to hitch a little shrug. Whether it hits the mark on the nonchalance I am aiming for is hard to discern—especially because *his* face has transformed to the opposite. I avoid that new intensity to explain, "You...sounded busy. I did not want to be..."

I let it trail off as he enters the stall, seeming to do so in one masterful sweep. I am sure he opened the glass door, even stepped over the tile lip at the shower's edge, but those sort of movements always seem to simply flow into the powerful prose of his body...

And now the unblinking force of his stare.

"You did not want to be what?"

His tone, just as unflinching, pulses more parts of me to life again. But we are discussing his conversation with Rob, and recalling that brings back composure. At least a little. "In the way," I supply. "Or interfering...with...important subjects."

A worm on a hook would be more graceful. I am certain my face flushes, beyond what color the steam has already brought. The man is no bloody help, tilting my face up with a finger and then softly but thoroughly kissing me. Before I can help it, my arms twine around his neck, my body molds against every gloriously hard inch of him—only, when I expect him to swoop in with the full force of his lust, he steps back. Then again. Literally looks down to make sure his lengthening sex is not touching me in any way before finally speaking again.

"Let's make something clear." He jogs his head in the direction of the bedroom. "*That* is all the 'interference.' *That's* all the 'getting in the way' crap. *This*"—he traces a finger in the air between our chests—"and *this*"—and then between our foreheads—"is the 'important subject' you need to be worrying about."

I only swallow hard. There is nothing to say. And everything. And I am more flummoxed than ever.

"Mishella."

"What?"

"Look at me." His stare awaits, ready with forest darkness. "Yeah. I thought so."

"Thought so...what?"

"You don't believe me."

"Because I do not *have* to." I grab his hands. "Cassian, you had a life before I arrived. And you shall have one after I leave—"

"So you're already that anxious to go?" The forests flare with angry fires. I try to understand—anger is fear's child, so what is he afraid of?—but cannot surpass my own uncertainty to see it. I am thousands of miles from home, in a land where even the stupid light switches are new to me, and *he* is playing at the jilted insecurity?

"Are you truly asking that?" I seethe. "After the last three days? After I gave you my *virginity*?"

"Which I paid for," he retorts, "as *you* cannot seem to stop reminding me."

"Because it is the truth!"

"Because that 'truth' is your safety."

He does not stop at the accusation. Uses his body as judge and juror, convicting me with the physical lunge that not only closes the gap between us but flattens me against the shower's granite wall. His body, tightening and flexing, is now a hard, imposing intruder. His shoulders bunch, ropes of muscles playing against his wet flesh, as he meshes our fingers against the granite.

"Look at me," he growls again. "Look. At. Me." When I do, he lowers his face until I can see my reflection in the beads of water down his straight nose, along his clenched jaw. "You don't get to be safe here, Ella. Neither of us does. We can keep talking about the money, keep pretending it's the chasm that's protecting our castles—or we can just admit the truth." His hands screw tighter into mine. His body pushes harder... so much bigger... "I'm *in* the fucking chasm, woman—and I'm careening. Tumbling. Every moment I'm with you, next to you, inside you, it gets deeper. Darker. There's no bottom in sight—nor do I want there to be."

I work to get air. Very little comes. My balance tilts. My senses swim. He is the only anchor—my new reality. I whimper, lost in the force of his rough words...the magic. Wanting to believe magic really exists...

but...

"Wh-What about...her?"

His gaze glitters. He shakes his head, confused. "Her *who*?"

Before the answer is even out, I feel like a petty salpu. "Amelie," I clarify, feeling as if I must. "Hampton. Remember? The woman who responds on your behalf to social engagements?"

"Because she was torqued at me for going to Arcadia without her. Because she also doesn't know how to express herself like, let's say, a mature adult." He pulls away. His shoulders dip as if a weight has been slung across them. "And also, because I've let her get away with it before." Measured huff. "Look...I won't lie to you, Ella. I've let several women get away with it before—because I haven't really cared before."

My turn for the irked exhalation finally comes. "So...what does that mean..."

...*for me.*

I let the words remain implied. He is not a stupid man. He shows me so by settling his gaze firmly back into mine. "It means that I care now." He lets go of my hands, closing them both in to frame my face. "That I'm not going to that goddamn event with anyone on my arm but the most beautiful woman in New York." His dimples reappear, deep as craters, as I crunch a questioning frown. "*You*, my *pahaleur* armeau."

For the first time in my life, I roll my eyes at a man.

Partly because he deserves it.

Partly because I know I can.

Mostly because it feels so, *so* good.

In return, his own eyes go dark with sage smoke. "Christ. Did you roll your eyes at me?" When I do it again, the desire takes over the rest of his face—and his cock slots against my most sensitive tissues, zinging heat to every nerve ending in my body. "You know what I want to do with that expression, don't you, young lady?"

The grate in his tone brings me more boldness. I toss a flirty glance up, tugging at my lip with my teeth—and his erection with my fingers. He hisses. I clutch harder. By the Creator, I love touching him. *Everywhere*—but especially here. Feeling him pulse beneath my palm. Watching his jaw clench. Savoring the power that I, for once, have over *him*...

"Hmmm," I murmur. "I...have no idea. Maybe it is best that you show me, Mr. Court?"

His throat vibrates with a low, snarly sound. "Maybe it's best that I do."

My breath clutches. Holds. I hope, perhaps too desperately, for my backside and the shower seat to become best friends again. Instead, Cassian shifts his hold to my shoulders, urging me down. The action is too brusque to let me trail him with kisses, but I am able to take a tactile exploration. My hand travels the hills of his abdomen, glides into the indent of his hip, savors the perfect plateaus of his thighs. "Beautiful," I rasp. "You are...so beautiful, Cassian."

He lifts his hands, burying them in the wet tangles of my hair, as I kneel before him. With his hold digging into my scalp, he grates, "Then wrap *your* beauty around me."

I cannot refuse. I do not want to. In my most illicit dreams I have already imagined doing this for him...and for me. Taking over him like this, hoping I can enthrall his body as he does mine... I am flushed all over, intoxicated and afire... All my senses swirl, aroused and alive.

"Fuck." His groan is as tight as the sinew of his legs, clenching as I grasp them, pushing him deeper inside me. His flesh, musky and wet, pushes at the confines of my mouth. So huge. So delicious. His hands brace the back of my head, soon setting a pace for each new lunge over his pulsing length. "Beautiful...*favori*...take me...take me..."

His words are like the steam, curling around us, dissolving my thoughts into nothing more than particles on the air. I've evaporated, now just a swirl myself, my actions completely controlled by his passion...his will.

"Touch yourself, Ella. Stroke your clit."

I obey at once. Release a moan around his girth.

"Touch *me* with your other hand. Around my balls. *Yes.* Like *that.*"

I moan louder. So does he. He rams into my mouth at a quicker pace. The sack beneath my hand throbs and writhes. His cock grows, testing the limits of my throat.

Faster.

Hotter.

Sucking.

Stroking.

Climbing.

Coming.

As the zenith hits my pussy, I scream—welcoming the ropes of cream he gives my throat. I drink burst after burst of his perfect completion...his beautiful passion. And embrace all the beauty he sees in *me* too...

And am glad the water cascading down our bodies can mask the sheen of my tears, born of an exquisite, inescapable realization.

In being owned by him...

I have been set truly free.

Leaving only one insane dilemma.

How will I ever set *him* free now?

CASSIAN

I have to turn from Ella while buttoning up my shirt.

First, the sight of her in the chair next to the window, dressed in nothing but my bathrobe, is too fucking tempting. She's only five feet from the bed I yearn to throw her back onto, keeping her captive for three more days.

Second—my fingers are shaking.

Trembling.

Me.

Like a fucking cat in the rain.

And I never want it to end.

The same way I never wanted to leave that bed. Or the shower—dear *fuck*, that shower—or the magical wrap of her arms, her eyes, her body.

How the hell am I ever going to set her free?

Because in another five months and three weeks, she'll be

properly purged, man. Spoiled and fucked into perfect oblivion. With any luck, she'll even be like all the rest: another Amelie, ready to stomp all over your space with the social engagements, the photo ops...perhaps even the pre-business trip hissy fits...

The argument has merit.

Except for one major snag.

I *like* thinking of Mishella Santelle in those scenarios. Yeah, even the hissy fit one. *If* there would ever be any need to leave her behind on a trip, and *if* she ever found the need to launch such a tantrum, defusing her anger might be more fun than stoking her passion. The woman's pretty damn adorable when she's miffed. Her gaze turns to blue fire, her neck cords with tension, and she turns all Queen Victoria proper, practically using the royal *we* on everybody.

We are mad at you, Mr. Court...

We would like you to keep sucking on our nipples...

We would like to suck on your cock...

We would enjoy coming for you...

Yep. Shaking.

I finish with the damn buttons. Not a miracle yet. That comes when I remember how to secure a Windsor knot...that is, when I recall where I put the fucking tie...

My search doesn't last long. It ends with a punch of violent feeling, at finding the strip of red silk trailing from elegant fingers that I long to kiss once more—and do. Ella's smile fills her eyes before her lips, a sequence reaffirming my newfound buy-in to Arcadian voodoo, before she loops the tie around my neck and focuses on the knot. I'm actually jealous of the thing, watching the attention it receives for the better part of a minute, until a more disturbing thought sets in.

"How'd you learn to do this?"

Translation: *what man did you learn it for?*

She smirks. My subtext isn't the subtlest, and I don't give a fuck. "My brother." She tugs softly, taking her time, and I sense the quiet intimacy of the moment means as much to her as me. "All the kids on Arcadia wear school uniforms until our last year of secondary level. Saynt never perfected his knot, at least not to Maimanne's satisfaction, so I just did the job and let her believe what she wanted."

More emotion wallops me. This time, fierce protectiveness. It pushes my hand up, clasping one of her wrists. When she looks up, I don't ease back on my probing stare. "Would an imperfect knot have been that much of a sin?"

I expect her to drop her gaze. When she doesn't, for a very long moment, she lets me see in...allows me to really view the panorama of her life up until now. It is filled with shifting sands, fickle winds, even a fear of where the next step may take her. Steps that have, until now, all been orchestrated by her parents—down to the threads in her and Saynt's clothing.

Finally, she looks away. Her arm drops too. "And perfection was not expected of *you*, Mr. Court?"

Clearly, my sadness has come off as pity—not a surprise, if the filter of her pride is considered—so her defensiveness isn't a shock. Nor is the logic behind her words. I've tracked her parents' "research" into Court Enterprises. Undoubtedly, they've told her I didn't inherit the money behind all this. In her mind, two and two are now snapped together—and sum up to a pair of demanding parents.

Little Ella. If only the world were so tidy.

"Perfection," I echo, arching a brow. "Of course it was expected of me. Every day."

She nods, face full of *I knew it.*

"By the guy in the mirror."

The nod halts. "But your mother—"

"Was usually at work by the time I got up for school." I square my shoulders. It's not a new move, even with the onslaught of those distant memories—things not even her parents' probe could have divulged about me. Mom prefers to let me live the public life and now enjoys the garden she never had while I was growing up, in her dream house out in Connecticut. The way it should be. "She had to take a bus and two trains to get to the Four Seasons on time for clock-in." I cock my head. "You know those rich New York farts. They all don't have much patience when their toilets have to be scrubbed."

She doesn't bite on the levity. Instead mutters, confused frown in place, "But your father surely—"

"Wasn't around." I manage to get it out smoothly.

"A brother or a sis—"

"Wasn't. Around." Not so smooth this time. By half. But Damon is nobody's business. Ever.

"So...it was just you?"

Yes. In an apartment smaller than this room, with the cocaine addicts on one side and the schizophrenic lady on the other. At least the crackheads were quiet in the mornings.

"This isn't the right time for this discussion, Ella."

She nods once more. The *I knew it* is gone, but I instantly wish for its return. Anything but the terse lurch into which the action has become. "Of course it is not. I...apologize."

"Dammit." I seethe it beneath my breath, to myself more than her, before wheeling back, grabbing her, and tucking her close. "No apologies," I utter into her hair. "Ghosts are just better left buried; that's all."

"I understand."

But she doesn't. Not really. After courageously unlocking her emotional gates for me, she has met padlocks and guard dog growls from me in return. Not a damn thing I'm going to do about it either.

I tried exposing the pain once before. Forced the gates open.

Was given just another ghost to bury.

Headstone carved with flowers to match her name...

Fresh dirt over the plot, contrasted by the February snow over the graveyard...

I grit the memories away. Gaze over the top of Ella's head, out the window. It's May, but the morning sky roils over the city, thick with thunderheads, as if even the big guy beyond them challenges my call. *Go ahead, bastard. Give it a try. You turned my secrets into sunshine once and then ripped the sun away. Now, the secrets stay with the ghosts. Buried. For good.*

I pull in a deep breath. Normally, it's enough for fortification. Not now. I dip my head, seeking the solace of her warmth, her kiss—but as soon as our mouths meet, I revise the descriptor. This isn't just solace. It's healing. She might hate that my gate is closed, but she accepts it...and simply fixes what she can from where I *do* let her stand.

She really is a gift.

I've never considered it hell to stop kissing a woman before. Today marks *that* first, giving new meaning to the words *fuck* and *no*. Somehow she deciphers it properly and giggles a little.

"Off with you, Mr. Court." She adjusts my tie one last time, giving me an accidental eyeful of her cleavage. "The sooner you get done ruling the world, the sooner you can come h—" She barely snatches back the rest, but it's enough to shatter our pretense of domestic bliss as she revises, "The sooner you can get back." She lifts a little smile over eyes turning rich turquoise. "And remember, you have a physician's appointment today."

Oh. Yes. That.

I step back, guiding her hands into mine—deciding to just broach the subject, now that she's gone there anyway. Clearly, the more "formal" moment for which I've been waiting is not coming soon—especially with her standing there, soft and scrubbed and naked in my robe.

"I had Rob make that appointment"—I deliberately engage her gaze—"for you."

Nose crinkle. Slow blink. "Me? What? Wh-Why?"

No better tactic than a direct one. "It's with Kathryn Robbe. She's a friend. And a gynecologist."

"A gyne—" She's confused more than upset. Good sign. "But Cassian, you know my history. Well, my lack of one. You are my first—"

I stop her with a kiss. It's as much for me as her. Hearing her speak it out loud, that I'm the only man who's ever been inside her, fires primeval urges I don't even want to subdue. After a long minute of claiming her with my tongue, I pull back far enough to speak my full, transparent intent.

"It's just to make sure everything's working fine, favori."

She spurts a little laugh. "After the last three days, you are not sure it is?"

"And to talk to Kathryn about birth control."

More blinks. But no more frowns. Just a gorgeous little O of her lips, followed by the same sound in a rasp. "Oh," she repeats. "You...errmm...that is what you want?"

I lower my head. Inhale deeply. Attempt to absorb the clinical scents between us, not the sensual. Toothpaste, deodorant, shirt starch—*not* body cream, vanilla soap, even the sexy place at the curve of her nape, where her citrus shampoo blends with beads of her perspiration. So many more places like this on her to discover. Marvelous places...

"What I *want*"—Christ, what I *need*—"is to get my body inside yours whenever and wherever I want." Her all-over shiver conveys I've made the point, but my imagination's off and running again. "For instance, I'd be able to tear this robe off of you. Kind of like...*this*."

"Oh." Her mouth is a rose around the syllable now...dark as the areolas sprouting her erect nipples. Her hair cascades around those lush swells, turning her into my very own Aphrodite...ready to be claimed by her worthless mortal once more. "And—and then what?"

The dusky cue in her gaze is all I need. "And then...I'd be able to spin you around and march you to the window seat." I twist her hair around a hand and push her forward. When we're in front of the bench built into the curve of the window, I angle her over until her cheek is pressed down—and her ass is presented high. "Like this."

"Oh...*my*." She wriggles a little, spreading her legs for better balance...exposing the tight entrance now gaping on the air, its glistening layers begging to be filled. Because denying myself air would be easier than rejecting her needs, I give the sorceress what she wants. With one finger, then two...and three. "Cassian!" she cries. "Oh, by the Creator..."

"If you were taking protection, Ella, I could unzip my pants...like this. Then pull out my cock...and line it up to your weeping little cunt..."

"Please," she begs when I only follow through with the first half of that promise. Instead, I let her listen as I fist my length and begin to pump, in perfect cadence with the three digits inside her sex. "*Please!*"

At first I say nothing, letting her arousal spiral with mine, continuing to fuck my fingers into her, keeping a perfect rhythm. But then I pivot my hand, letting my thumb hook up, toying with the rosette between her ass's perfect spheres. "I could play here, too...while I fuck your sweet pussy. Spread your gorgeous ass and then press into it...like this..."

The filthy scene, playing out in both our minds, brings on a mutual shudder. I delve my fingers deeper into her pussy... and her other entrance, so tiny and tight.

"Yes," she keens. "Oh, yes...take me..."

"In both places?"

"In both. I need it. I need *you*. Cassian...Cassian..."

There are more words, long strings of them, but the Arcadian spills from her in such a heated slur, I can only assume she's continuing the dirty theme. At least that's what my cock wants to believe. Engorged and pulsing, precome slicking the length, the beast roars through my fist, over and over again, screaming for release as desperately as Mishella does.

And Christ, does she scream.

Openly.

Gloriously.

"*Ardui! Faisi-banu-ardui!*"

I can translate only the last word, but it's enough.

Harder.

My enchantress's wish is my command.

We orgasm together, her gasps mating with my roar. Her walls squeeze around my fingers. My fist milks my cock.

Streams of my essence fall across her back, like white chocolate poured against vanilla ice cream. Though I am spent, the sight of it keeps me hard...craving to lean over and fill her with my dick instead of my fingers.

Instead, as our breathing normalizes, I force myself to step back. Scooping my robe back up, I improvise it into a towel, cleaning her back and my cock before scooping her back up against me...yearning to hold her like this all damn day.

Well, not exactly like this.

Doing it in bed would be so much better. Naked and sated, limbs twined, heads sharing a pillow...

For a moment, I consider it. Strongly. Nothing sounds better right now than fucking the day's demands—but even amenable Rob will point out that canceling on Flynn Whelan is professional poison. The man has clout with both the Greek and Croatian governments, contacts we'll be needing once operations in Arcadia move forward in full force. And right now, staying close to the Arcadians has leapt high on my priorities list.

Close.

It's never felt like a flimsy word—but right now, drawing Ella even closer, it comes nowhere near to what I crave to share with her...what I still burn to have beyond this. I've just compared her to a decadent dessert and stuffed my senses full of the damn thing, yet I'm ravenous for more. So much more.

But will it ever be enough?

I hope so.

Dear fuck, I hope not.

The breath I fan into her neck is full of that rough conflict. She responds with a quiver, rolling down through her whole body, making her skin pebble beneath my touch. I firm my roaming caresses, partly to warm her, partly to memorize the feel of her nakedness. *Something* has to get me through the day, goddammit.

She finally breaks our silence with a hitched murmur. "Cassian?"

I wrapped myself tighter around her. "Yeah?"

"I will go to the appointment. With your friend."

I tilt my head in. Press lips to her temple. "Thank you, armeau."

She cocks her own head. There's an impish smile on her lips. "You can thank me later. In *very* thorough detail."

I growl lowly. "Yes, ma'am." Then set about proving how I fully intend to follow through—by stealing that smile off her lips with the attack of my own.

CHAPTER NINE

MISHELLA

Scott drops me off at the front door of Kathryn Robbe's medical office, which is attached to her home somewhere in a neighborhood on the other side of Central Park. It is far from the sterile environment I spent the morning dreading, and I am more relaxed than I ever thought possible—under the circumstances. There is even a little cartoon bubble taped to the ceiling overhead, emblazoned with the words *I Hate This*. It eases the discomfort, perhaps a little, of having my womb examined from the inside out.

"Okay, then. All finished." Her tone is crisp but friendly as she pulls out the speculum, and I release my breath in a relieved whoosh. Does any woman ever "breathe normally" through a pelvic exam? "Why don't you get dressed and then join me in the other room?"

"Of course."

The "other room" is a cozy office reminding me a little of similar spaces in Palais Arcadia at home. The furniture is just as grand, though made of darker woods. A pair of Turkish carpets overlap on the polished wood floor. Bookshelves line an entire wall, and the big desk looks like the workspace of a busy but happy person.

A few elements *not* like home: the pair of plush chairs

in the center of the room, also formed of dark wood but cushioned in cream velvet. The upholstery matches the colors of an ornate tea table, centered between the chairs.

"Do you like tea?" Her eyes, the color of sherry, smile as much as her lips. Her hair, pulled into a stylish French twist, is almost the same hue. She would be described as a handsome woman and looks enough like Cassian that she could pass as his older sister. "If not, I can grab some lemonade from the fridge." She motions to a kitchenette, off to my left.

"Tea is fine." I smile as I sit, folding my hands in my lap and crossing my ankles. "And those cookies look even better." There have to be at least three dozen of the assorted confections, arranged on a multi-tiered tray.

"Ohhhh. Someone else with a sweet tooth." She winks. "Cas told me I'd like you."

Cas?

I hide the jealous spike with an answering smile. "Thank the Creator I ate a filling lunch." A salmon filet, served by a sedate Prim—who has decided to warm to my presence, inch by agonizing inch. I think she even stopped scowling, for a flash, when I complimented her about the meal.

"Well, these are light. And calories consumed during business don't count." She shrugs and chuckles. "And I kept the lab coat on, so we can consider this business, right?"

I try not to smile too brightly. If she only knew how close to "business" this really is for me. Or maybe...she *does* know. By the powers, how much information has "Cas" supplied her with?

I lick my lips. Decide to borrow a gutsy page from Vy's book, and "suck it up" with the direct approach. It is not graceful—but sometimes in life, one simply cannot be.

"So...exactly what *is* your relationship with...*Cas*?"

She concludes a sip of tea. To my pleasant surprise, gives a smiling nod. "Bull by the horns. Now I *really* like you."

That is not my answer, but I feel far from pressured to point it out. Sure enough, as soon as the woman finishes nibbling a pink macaron, she replies, "Do you mean am I a lover? Or an ex?"

I take a fortifying bite of cookie for myself. To quote my best friend again, *Gawd...delish.* "I suppose that *is* what I mean."

Once more she nods, that *atta girl* sparkle in her oh-so-American eyes. "The answer is no and no," she offers. "I went to college with Cassian. We went on one date, which nearly ended in disaster."

I scowl. "How so?"

"Depends on who you ask: him or me."

"Well, *you* are sitting here."

"But *he's* at the front of your mind." She arches knowing brows at my confirmation of a blush. "Long story short, the man is too damn serious."

I practically choke on my next bite of cookie. "You are speaking of...Cassian? Cassian *Court*?" The man with the charm that will not stop captivating me? With the smile that will not let up on assaulting my heart and the laugh that flips my stomach each time it takes over his lips?

"Six-foot-three? Eyes like the Emerald City skyline? Hair so perfect, it belongs on a kid half his age auditioning for a boy band? *That* Cassian Court?"

We laugh together. That is a very good thing, since it disguises my urge to wistfully sigh at her description instead. I finish with a curious cock of my head. "And yet...you fought with him on your first date."

"On our *only* date." She settles back a little farther, crossing her legs at the knee and absently circling her raised ankle. "Half of one, at that—thank God." An impressive eye roll gets inserted. "All that damn intensity in one man. He was out to set the world on fire before we were able to legally drink. 'Relax' definitely wasn't a word in his vocabulary, even with dorky bowling shoes on his feet and beer disguised as soda in his hand."

"Bowling...shoes." A frown sets in before I can help it. Racking my brain for the Arcadian translation of the word equates to a blank screen—but this "bowling" must be important. They even have special shoes for it.

Kathryn breaks into another laugh. "Hard to believe, right? The man of Kiton and Berluti, kickin' it casual with a girl in a beat-up bowling alley on a Friday night?" She rests her head against a raised hand. "Neither could he."

"Ambition is not an awful thing." I almost cannot believe the words are coming out—even in defense of Cassian. Firsthand, I have seen ambition's toll on a person—*two* of them—and on a marriage that was really never a marriage. But thanks to Cassian and the benefits of *his* drive, I shall never be prisoner to that loveless cage. It is all my choice now—and in a flash, I recognize there is a good chance I will never choose it. Not if I cannot have—

What?

What you have with Cassian? What you are only going to have for six months?

Forever is a long time to be alone, Mishella.

"Of course it's not." The woman's murmur, lined with sincerity, saves me from the miserable turn of my thoughts.

"But in this city, it's a drug as lethal as crack or meth—in some cases, more addictive."

I swallow hard—letting my mind follow her lead. Hating myself for every step into that dark, uncomfortable place. "In Cassian's case?"

She barely blinks before answering quietly, "I was starting to fear it...yes."

"Why?"

At that, she *does* blink. "I think he's still purging demons."

I gulp again. No use. My throat is tight and dry—because I feel the truth of her words. I *know* it. "Wh-What demons?"

Kathryn lowers her leg. Scoots forward. Pulls in both elbows to her knees. Murmurs as if apologizing, "They're not my stories to tell. And I don't even know all of them. But... they're there, Mishella. Spurring him. Haunting him." The faraway lilt in her voice is suddenly counteracted...by the new smile edging her lips. "Well, they *were*. Until today."

I straighten. "Huh?"

"Until today," she repeats. "Actually, just an hour ago—when he called, right before you got here, and all but ordered me to take great care of you."

Tiny zings of pride and warmth chase each other through my chest. "Oh," I blurt.

"Yeah," she returns, adding a new chuckle. "*Oh*. The man who never *attempted* his bossy-boss act with me since the bowling alley catastrophe..." The chuckle mellows. "But now, because of you, he's pulled out his full Smokey the Bear again. It gives me hope."

I don't even hear her last words. "He has a *bear*?" I recall the moment, in Paipanne's study, back on the island. He had offered to buy me a dog but said nothing about—

"Why don't we make sure he doesn't have a cow, much less a bear." She returns to her soft laughter, clearly proud of herself for the "humor," but sobers when I cannot even feign understanding of the line. Not for the first time in my life, I yearn for a transplant into Vylet's body. The woman is able to laugh even at watching grass grow—and actually has.

"Most excellent of plans."

It is cheerful enough to earn my "game face" as punctuation, seeming to center Kathryn too. Back into doctor mode, she rises—literally—standing with brisk efficiency. "Well, I think *you're* an excellent plan, at least where it concerns my friend Cassian." The strange shadows flit across her gaze again. "He's been by himself for far too long."

I return to my feet as well. "But...surely I am not the first 'friend' he has sent to see you."

She does not placate me with a denial, which would also be a lie. But what she does say is just as huge a seed for disconcerting thoughts—and even deeper emotions.

"Giving a man 'friends' for his body doesn't do a damn thing for his soul." She pulls in a prolonged breath. "And fighting off the *alone* doesn't mean you're taking care of the *lonely*."

The words dig into the sides of my mind, refusing to leave even after Kathryn handles the "business" of why I have come and then wraps our visit with a heartfelt hug. It clings as she taps her "digits" into the new cell phone Cassian has purchased for me—and even during her invitation for a "girls' lunch" soon. Though her kindness imparts me with needed confidence, the dark disquiet about Cassian continues to creep in.

Intensity. Ghosts. Lonely.

Beneath the man's rapier swagger and ruthless business

cunning, is he truly a haunted beast in a solitary tower? And what—or who—put him there?

The queries overshadow even my awe about New York's nonstop pageantry as Scott drives me back to Temptation—only the trip seems exceedingly short. As we roll to a stop, I peer through the tinted windows in wonder. We are not back at the house. Instead, I look out at wide cement sidewalks, buildings blocking the very sun, and edges of chrome and glass everywhere.

"Errrmm...Scott?"

But Scott is no longer in the driver's seat. He suddenly appears, having opened the limo's back door, extending a hand to help me out...

Onto the sidewalk before a set of massive glass doors... gliding open like the gates of a modern palace...

Court Towers
Court Enterprises Incorporated

...with its very own, breath-stealing king.

My lungs cease working at the mere sight of him. That transforms the journey toward him into an interesting experience—knees liquid, heart thudding, palms gummy—while my gaze works to connect a single thought within my brain.

I was naked with that king. Four hours ago. In his bed. In his shower. On his window seat...

The memories lend me fortitude. I need it. I must attempt a feat so outside my comfort zone, only borrowed words from Vy explain it.

Sizing up my competition.

I have always hated the vulgar words, but right now, there

is no better phrase for the dozen women and three men who are just as fixated on Cassian as I am—who, I am certain, lust after the same experience I do. To explore the proud body beneath that luxurious suit. To dive fingers into that thick honey hair. To learn if the glints in those emerald eyes are really hints of deeper, hotter desires...

Perfect timing for *that* thought. Cassian surely reads it in my eyes as we approach each other—then again while taking my hands and yanking me close. Now our bodies are nearly flush...and I almost think he will follow through with a crushing kiss.

For a moment, even here, I wish he would.

Instead, with a tight grunt, he behaves. Lowers his face until only I am privy to his quiet murmur, delivered from barely moving lips. "Dear fuck, armeau. Does that light in your eyes mean what I hope it does?"

I giggle. Just for a moment. "You mean the desire I share with nearly every other woman in this lobby?" Stolen glance one way, then the next. "And a few of the men too."

"Sucks to be them." His fingers twist tighter around mine. His stare dips to my lips. "Because the only thing I can think about is where to get you private and alone."

"I am certain Flynn Whelan might find *that* an interesting show."

He growls and then huffs. "The only 'show' Flynn Whelan cares about is the Canine Classic."

"The...what?"

"Dogs," he explains. "Greyhounds, to be exact. They're his only passion besides his businesses." His gaze swoops down again, teasing tingling energy into the bodice of my pink cotton dress. "But if you're that into putting on a show...we can talk later on tonight."

I sigh as his head lifts again. His gaze is a thousand shades of thrilling, so many verdant colors colliding. I am a heated, pulsing mess, craving the audacity to pull him close and then plead for one of his thrilling bites on my neck...

"*Behave.*" I issue it to myself as much as him. We force ourselves back to the respectable hand hold—though his eyes remain hooded, and I can see his clenched teeth past the slight part in his lips.

When a long minute passes without him adding anything verbally, I prompt, "So..."

His dimples make an appearance. *Heart. Thud.* "So?"

"Ummm...why am I here, Cassian?" I resist adding a crack about showing me his etchings. The man is likely to take me seriously—and I refuse to be the reason for him missing the key meeting with Flynn Whelan.

"Does there have to be a reason?"

Heart. Thunk. And...mortifying blush. "I...I guess not."

"Guess I just needed to see that," he murmurs.

"See what?"

"That blush." His thumbs brush my knuckles. "I've missed it."

A discreet laugh sneaks past my lips. "As Vylet would say, Mr. Court...you are full of shit."

"Good thing my cock isn't already half-hard for Vy, then."

Heart. Melt. Taking the rest of my body with it.

"How'd everything go with Kathryn?"

"Good." I sound breathless and smitten. Who am I fooling? I *am* breathless and smitten. And now that the subject has shifted to us soon being able to act on our lust anywhere we want...a little sheepish. "Good, good," I rush out. "Everything is...errrmm...working fine. And safely." I already know he is. Even the memory of holding his clean lab results rushes more heat to my face. I must be the color of a ripe tomato by now.

Cassian shifts a little closer. "Did she...give you a prescription?"

"Better." I lift a coy smile. "An injection."

"Ah. Good...good." He sounds as flustered as I am, but when he lets out a long exhale, the force of his lust possesses every molecule of the air. "*Ella.*"

"Y-Yes?"

"How soon can I be bare inside you?"

My gaze is snatched back up to his. My whole mouth goes dry. Somehow, I manage the response. "T-Twenty-four hours."

His hands slide to the backs of my elbows. His stare returns to its green fire, razing into me...through me. By the Creator, my thighs clench at its incursion. My sex throbs, feeling weighted but empty. *So empty.* Especially after he leans in, whispering words so molten, I am grateful he supports my wobbly walk to the car afterward.

"Twenty-four hours. And starting now, I'm counting every fucking minute."

★ ★ ★

It only takes ten minutes to drive from Court Towers to Temptation—but in that time, I must swing through just as many emotions. Everything from desire, need, and teen girl-style giddiness is mixed with a soul-deep recognition of the ghosts Kathryn so eloquently explained to me earlier. Of course I have observed the darkness in Cassian's eyes before; I simply have been lacking a way of identifying them...perhaps even seeking an excuse for them, like extended jet lag or simply deep-seated concern about business matters.

No more pretending now.

No more simple veils or innocent oversights.

But Kate has given me no more to go on. *They're not my stories to tell, Mishella.*

And yet, confronting Cassian about them was simply not an option during our ten minutes together—in glaring public. Letting him make goo-goo eyes at me was one thing; bringing up Kate's cryptic words another. A *huge* "another."

So now I stand, in the middle of his home, knowing what I know—but unable to do anything about it. Knowing that there are, in Kate's words, things that have *haunted* him so wholly, he has been obsessed with nothing but work excellence and professional success...

For how long?

For what reasons?

And to what purpose?

In the last week, I have locked stares with the man so many times, there is no more counting them. Every time, it is the closest I have felt to twining my soul with another's...to knowing the heart that is also my own. When I take him inside my body, it is like welcoming *myself* home...a shore drawing the tide close...

Has it all been an illusion?

Do I not *know* Cassian Court at all?

And how, in the space of just a week, can I not bear to live with that information as my truth?

Hodge and Scott are downstairs, detailing the cars— Cassian owns three more besides the Jaguar, all prettier and more demanding of upkeep—and Prim is in the kitchen, baking things that make me want to declare dinner will be nothing but dessert tonight. I use the solitude to wander the rooms of the main living floor...not knowing what I plan to find but hoping it will be *some* kind of clue about the secrets Cassian keeps behind such high walls in himself.

With every step, I battle myself.

You met him a week *ago.*

"A week in which our lives have completely changed," I defend in a whisper.

Most couples barely know each other's middle names after a week.

"We are not a couple." I smile from that one. My inner Vylet even high-fives me for it.

He will not even share every secret with Kathryn.

"And the silence is shredding him!"

My whisper has not made it any less a melodrama—making me wonder why I still cannot laugh about it. Perhaps that is because of the twisting, deep in my belly, confirming that even melodrama can carry truth.

The thought gives me conviction. I walk through each room once again, searching for the tiniest sliver of understanding about who Cassian Court really is. About the secrets that don't just motivate him...

They're there, Mishella...haunting him...

I still find nothing.

I peer harder at the sleek walls, glass accents, and elegant furniture, all seemingly custom-crafted for each of his main living spaces. Every inch practically screams of the money spent on it—and the effort expended to separate it from the scrollwork and romance of the building's exterior. Even the décor pieces are carefully crafted to fit the look: slick, clean, neutral.

None of it matches *him.*

Not the man I have talked with, laughed with, opened up to, and seen into for the last three days. Not the person to whom I feel more connected than anyone in my life, including Vy and Saynt. Not the lover who has given me himself in return—or so I have thought.

I have sensed them...those missing pieces of him... or rather, felt the empty spaces in him sometimes. The unexplained moments of stillness. The searching casts of his gaze, toward a horizon that does not exist...maybe for a person who is no longer there.

Ghosts.

Spurring. Haunting.

I should be patient. Let *him* come to *me*, in his time...

But he has known Kathryn since college—nearly ten years—and he still only gives *her* the shadows.

I cannot accept the shadows.

Ella...it's time to live in the light.

I want his light too.

I have six months with him, not ten years.

Fortune favors the brave.

It feels like destiny to remember the words, a favorite expression often used by King Evrest back home. Evrest even credits their importance in helping his journey toward true love—though that is far beyond my ambition right now and must remain that way.

It must *remain that way.*

I have no idea where Cassian and I are bound with each other. I only know that he has helped me at least see my light— and now, if I can help him step toward his too...

Determinedly, I search the spaces again. Living room.

Game room. Movie theater. All three guest bedrooms. Even the gym. Still nothing. No mementos from travels, nor artwork that is not abstract. No knickknacks that are not completely curated or more than a few years old, and everything in sync with the out-of-a-movie décor.

I only find one photo, atop the desk in the study that is as sterile as a research laboratory. The image depicts a younger Cassian, between childhood and adulthood, probably twelve or thirteen. He hugs a woman with the same thick gold hair and piercing green eyes. If she is not his mother, I am the Queen of Persia.

Is *she* one of his ghosts?

I lower into one of the chairs in front of the desk—the leather is so stiff, I wonder if my backside is the first to ever touch it—and stare at the picture, fighting a helpless despair.

"Tell me what to do," I whisper to the woman in the photo. "I am certain I want the same thing as you. I just want him to be...happy."

Deep inside, I wish her sweet smile would order me to leave everything alone. But it does not. It delves to something even deeper...confirms what my gut has already told me since the conversation with Kate.

Satisfying his body comes nowhere close to reaching his soul.

To do that, I must find the ghosts.

"But where?" I beseech it of the room itself now, sending the plea upward as my head falls back. I close my eyes and loll the gray matter to the left. Reopen them...

To find my focus yanked like a weight across a thread. Pulled out the study's entrance, across the central hall, through the breadth of the living room...

To the handle of a door.

Leading to the stairway up to Turret Two.

I know this as a fact because there's an identical door on the other side of the living room—the one Cassian *has* led me through, that will forever hold one of the best memories of my life. But he has all but commanded me to forget Turret Two, dismissing it as "the joint's required junk room." Like a proper, smitten lover, I believed him. I still do.

But is not *junk* often another word for *the past*?

And in the past, there are ghosts.

I rise. My heart pounds at the base of my throat. This is it. The *X* on the treasure map.

On quiet steps, I cross to the door. Half expect it to be locked. Exhale in relief when it is not.

The air beyond the portal is different than that of Turret One. Chilled and dusty, though my feet do not leave any imprints on the wooden stairs as I start to climb. *Thank the Creator.*

But there *are* creaks.

I wince, wondering why I did not notice the sounds when ascending the other turret. *Because you were not trying to sneak someplace you do not belong?*

A scowl replaces the wince. Cassian has not expressly "forbidden" me to come up here. And I am *not* "sneaking." I am searching. There is a difference...

Which thoroughly explains why I jump like a criminal as someone rushes up the stairway behind me. Why my blood turns to ice and my cheeks flame with accusation as Prim's infuriated form comes into view.

"What the *hell* do you think you're doing?"

CASSIAN

"Mishella. What the hell were you doing?"

I clench my jaw to stop the query from spilling into accusation. She's already been subjected to that treatment; a minute into the phone call from Prim has betrayed that much already. While still on the line with her, I'd ordered Rob to cancel the rest of my day and used the Court Enterprises on-call car to get home, instead of waiting for Scott and the Jag.

Wasn't fast enough.

Prim's wrath has already taken its toll. I see it along the taut slashes of Ella's shoulders, in every glimmering sapphire surface of the gaze she'll no longer lift to mine. Instead, she stares across the study and out the window, perched on the edge of that damn chair—reminding me all too much of how stiff and scared she'd been back on Arcadia, that morning when I'd returned with the new contract.

Only now, she's afraid of me.

My jaw clamps harder. I get down a hard inhalation, battling the bizarre twist in my gut: the beginning of a tornado so distinct, it startles me as much as it terrifies me. I've only endured the tornado twice before. Once for Damon, once for Lily. This...*thing*...with Mishella is nothing like either of those times.

Is it?

I drop my head. Pinch my nose so hard, vessels are likely broken. I can only hope. A bloodbath from my nose is a thousand times better than a hemorrhage from my soul— which this *cannot* be. Not after a goddamn week...

You sure about that?

Are you absolutely *sure that seven days ago, you didn't*

walk into that reception hall on Arcadia, behold this woman, and feel every tangle in your brain fall free? Every sprint of your spirit reach its finish line...every hunger of your heart find its fill?

Hasn't everything since then...just made sense?

Except...that it doesn't.

"I—I just wanted to know more about you, Cassian."

And dammit, how it should.

If she were with any other man, it *would*.

"I know." Both words are growled, drenched in my defeat. *I hate this.* Hate that the secrets I must keep have made *her* feel like the one on trial here. I hate that Prim has become so obsessed with keeping those secrets, she's turned into the Temptation guard dog. I hate that she and Ella aren't up on the terrace right now, drinking wine and giggling about—whatever the hell women giggle about. Probably their men. In that case, Prim's giggles should be about Hodge, and Ella's should be about—

Not you, asshole.

But the thought of any other man making her smile, much less giggle, turns my ire into barely contained rage—an anger I have no goddamn right to. She's mine for only six months, and there's no room in that timeline for dredging up ghosts. She'll go back to Arcadia with memories of fire, passion, magic, and romance, *not* with the miserable stories of how fate, helped by two drug addicts I was stupid enough to love, has fucked my ability ever to trust words that mean even more than those. Words like *commitment*. And *promises*.

And *forever*.

Words she fully deserves in her life.

Not the goddamn misery. Or worse, her pity.

Sure as hell *not* with the story of how my wife threw

herself out Turret Two's window—and how I haven't been able to leave her ghost behind for four damn years.

She sneaks another furtive glance up at me. Squirms but sits straighter, like Lily herself is lurking nearby and gleefully wiggling the phantom flagpole up Ella's spine.

"I...I am sorry, Cassian."

"It's all right."

She stands in a rush. "No."

"Ella, really—it's all right."

"I mean *no*, I am not sorry."

Her fists bunch, pulling at the hem of the sweater she must've changed into when returning from Kathryn's—and visiting me. Best five minutes of my fucking day. Her lips twist, but she firms them before jogging up her chin once more.

"I—I am starting to...care about you, Cassian. Probably... more than I should." She works a bare toe against the floor— making me long to reach up, strip the gray leggings from her, and screw the rest of her unsteady questions right out of her eyes. Yeah, right here. Yeah, right now.

"I care about you too." My hands drop into their own tight balls. My jaw tautens again. None of it goes undetected by her darting gaze. By now, she has to discern the bottom line. I'm dancing around the real subject as much as she is. "Yeah," I finally add. "Probably more than I should."

Another damn placeholder. I've never just "cared" about this woman—unless the term encompasses a connection so strong, every circuit of my psyche has felt snapped into hers from the moment our eyes first met. Our mainframes completely synched...

Without any backup drive in place.

Fuck. So dangerous.

"So why is it a crime to want to know you better?"

"It isn't." When her brows jump, I emphasize, "It *isn't*. Prim reacted the way she did out of—"

"Love?"

I square my shoulders. "Yes." Pull in another breath. "Out of love. But not in the way you think." Hell. Could I get any more cliché? The sad answer is yes, because now I have to attempt an explanation about the bond to Prim without ripping back the scab over the wound named Lily. "You know the funny bit girls have, about friends being a rose garden?" When she gives a small nod, I finish, "Well, Prim and I aren't a garden. We're a briar patch. We both bleed a lot—"

"But it would hurt worse to leave."

Is it a shock that she concludes the thought so perfectly? Rhetorical question. It's also no news alert when my chest clenches from the aftermath: the look on her face depicting the briar thorns she's clearly still picking free from her spirit.

Dammit.

I need to fix this.

Disconnecting the mainframe isn't an option.

"Ella—"

"*Cassian.*" She takes a measured step back. "I—I understand, all right?" Her gaze turns dark and watery. "You have had years with her. I have had barely a week. She was right in reminding me of my place."

"Your *place*?" I rush forward. She retreats again, nearly skittering now. *Real smooth, idiot.*

"It is fine. Truly."

"No." The boulder in my chest is now a quarry, piled with chunks of tension. "Ella...*no*. Your place here..." I barely hold back from even reaching for her. "You belong in *every* place." *I

Because as far as I've let her in...

she can't be allowed to go all the way.

"That's...my mother." I feel my lips kick up as I lift the frame. "Her name is Mallory." I trace a finger around Mom's face. "She lives in Connecticut now, in a little place I bought her, with a garden and room for her cats."

"But this was not taken in Connecticut."

Still not a damn thing wrong with the sorceress's instinct. Right now, because things are still easy, I give her what she wants. "No. Not Connecticut. This was taken at the Jersey shore."

Suddenly, I'm there again. Maybe it's the way Ella always smells a little like the sea or the memories-on-demand corner I'm in, but for one incredible moment, I'm just a kid again, on a grand adventure with my mom and big brother...

"We were there on vacation," I murmur. "Just something last-minute Mom threw together. She did shit like that all the time." I laugh softly as the recollection takes deeper root. "We stayed in this...*dump*... Christ, the walls were so thin, we heard everything the couple next door was doing. Let's just say I got a crash course in the birds, the bees, and the entire animal kingdom."

"Oh, my."

For a moment, I simply gaze at the new flags of color across Ella's cheeks. *She steals my fucking breath.* "Oh, yeah. Probably the best two nights of my life up to that point." When she smacks my shoulder, I laugh. "Hey, you wanted to know!"

When her nose crinkles, my breath returns—in time to ignite my chest's fucking fireworks show. "Indeed I did. But I believe the proper term here is...TMI?"

"Too Much Information?" I slide a sly smirk. "Nah. Too

much information is bragging that my arm-fart of the national anthem kicked ass all over Damon's. Even Mom agr—"

The abort button is five seconds too late. Ella's curiosity is already in full bloom, though it's still the open, did-I-miss-something kind, not the what-the-hell-are-you-hiding kind.

"Damon?" Her innocence cinches the fresh twist in my gut. *Dammit*, was I really that careless? "Who is that?"

For a second—maybe more than one—I weigh the merit of a simple lie. *Simple? Really? How?*

Fine. Maybe half the truth. *He went with us to Jersey a few times. I was close to him in childhood.*

Both statements are completely true. But neither is the full truth.

"He was my brother."

And sometimes it's just better to lie in the fucking bed one makes.

She would've learned this part sooner or later. Something would've given her more than a passing clue, and then she'd mention it to her 'net-savvy little friend over in Arcadia, who'd hunt deeper than the basic wiki and biography websites from which Legal has managed to suppress the information so far. This way, I'm controlling the feed—and exactly how much of my soul is lobbed off in the doing. The wound will be repairable. A more invisible scar after she's gone.

"Your...brother." Her murmur is dotted with bewilderment. "Oh. I—I did not know—"

"Few do." My stomach clenches by another notch. I cloak the discomfort in a haven cold but familiar: the corporate photo pose. Powerful lean against the desk. One hand braced against the top, knuckles down. It says impenetrability. It says *back the hell down.*

But to someone like Mishella Santelle, it only says *here's your pause for more questions.*

"Well, does he live in Connecticut now too? Is he older or younger than you?"

And fuck it, all my heart wants to do is answer—as my soul screams from the incision.

"Older," I finally grit. "By two years." My fist grinds so hard against the desk, I expect cracks to fissure the glass plane. "At least...he was."

Her breath clutches—the sound I've been dreading. And now hate.

"W-Was?"

I twist my lips. Focus my stare out the window, onto something as innocuous as possible. A crow sits atop a chimney half a block away, a black sentinel against the late-afternoon sky. Why is that bird so still? And aren't crows supposed to be magical symbols of something?

"Cassian?"

I swivel toward her. It's torture, but I'm unable to fight it. *Magic.* It's not in the crow; it's right here in her searching gaze, her quiet concern, her soft sorrow...

No. Not sorrow.

Pity.

Fuck.

I am the subject of nobody's pity.

"This isn't something I want to talk about anymore, Mishella."

Her throat vibrates on a heavy swallow. Still, her chin jolts up before she replies, "Is that why the only sound louder than your fist against that desk is the grind of your teeth? Why you look as if you yearn to collapse where you stand but run as fast as you can at the same time?"

I jerk upright. Shove to my full stance. Pivot away. "This conversation isn't going to happen. Period."

I had to go and nickname her after the princess who walked home from the ball carrying a pumpkin and a bunch of mice. Her hand, persistent and elegant, wraps around my forearm from behind. "I think this conversation is long overdue."

"Then you think really wrong."

"I do not want to hurt you."

A laugh twists out of my constricting throat. "Christ, Mishella." All too fast, the laugh becomes a moan. "Don't you see?" I focus outside again—seeking the crow. Needing it to get out in a snarl, "You. Will. Incinerate. Me."

Pumpkin. Mice. This damn tenacious woman flattens herself against my back, her cheek like a flare to my whole spine...my whole being. "Maybe it is simply time to live in the light again."

Her arms circle my waist. She feels so fucking good...

I clutch her wrists. Bring her in closer. "But you like the dark better."

"Maybe the world needs both."

The husk in her voice follows the fiery path she has already ignited...up my spine and then back down. Spreading lower. Lower...

I shudder. She presses tighter.

"Cassian, please. I just want to help."

Her presence penetrates deeper. Makes me consider, if only for a moment...

What would it be like...to surrender? To really talk about it all? To let someone into the darkness again?

Like you let Lily in?

My breath rushes out, full of relief, as the thought slams in. It's the steel door I need. The clarity I crave. The passage back to the space I can best keep Ella too. Indeed, like a beacon, it guides my hands atop both of hers. Shoves them down until she's cupping me. The inferno of my thoughts turns into the perfect fire between my thighs.

"Then help me," I grate...pushing harder into her grip. Filling her fingers, which now follow my lead. She grips and sprawls and stretches, taking in the width of my bulge...

Her breath quickens against my back. "Oh. By the powers. *Oh.*"

"Yes. *Fuck*, yes..."

"No!"

It's just a gasp but breaks us apart like a scream. I wheel around but already know I shouldn't be—that my glare, spawned by disgust for myself, is going to look more like impatient fury. Like the expression of a man who expects to get his forty million dollars' worth out of the woman in front of him. The woman at whose feet he should be falling instead.

The woman who stumbles away, lips trembling, eyes entirely too bright.

"Well." Her chin jerks high again—while her hands wrestle in front of her stomach. "I suppose apologies are in order. I am...sorry, Cassian. Truly."

My throat squeezes. "What the hell? *You're* sorry?"

"You were right. This conversation really is not happening." Her eyes drop like a subject being judged by her king. "And now that I am enlightened about everything, it will not again. I give you my promise about that."

A strange weight slams my chest. "Promise?" I repeat. "Enlightened? I don't...understand."

"It is all right. *I* do." And why the hell is she *smiling* now—with such open serenity? "What you really wish for in all this is a bedmate."

"A bed *what*?"

"A fuck friend?" She cocks her head. "Is that more comfortable for you? Or do you prefer a calling booty?"

I unlock my teeth long enough to snap, "You are *not* my goddamn booty call."

"Hm." The sound is clipped as her smile taps out. She drops her head again—though not quickly enough. The shiny tracks on her cheeks are unmissable. "That is...an interesting point of view."

Another sensation invades my chest. It's not like the normal ache when I'm with her. It's worse—like my lungs are wrapped in rope and a dull knife is relentlessly sawing to get through. *Or to get out?*

"Mishella." The dagger's in my voice now, an entreaty for understanding. But will that matter? She wants things I can't give. She wants the past. She wants the truth.

She wants too much.

She lets my plea fall into silence as she turns and leaves on slow steps.

I watch until she disappears...

and then I can watch no more.

I spin back toward the desk, toward the window through which I crave to drive my fist—especially now with the crow on its sill, smugly eyeing me as darkness takes over the city behind him.

CHAPTER TEN

MISHELLA

"Black."

"Blue."

"And red all over?"

I watch, a little stunned, as my quip elicits the same wide eyes and dropped jaws from my two best friends. Their matched reactions are not strange because they have dialed into the video call from different locales in Arcadia but because they agree on something for the first time in thirty minutes. Granted, half that time has been spent studying the fifty evening gowns I have strewn across the largest of Temptation's guest rooms, and I am in the worst mood of my life *not* brought on by my parents, but the tension flowing from the two has been palpable—until now.

"Did she just...make a joke?" Brooke ventures.

Vylet cocks her head. "I think so."

"Everyone hold the line. I need to circle this day in red— somewhere."

"Hmmm. Maybe America *is* a good influence on you, missy thang."

I groan my way into a face palm. "Two weeks, Vy. I have been away for *two weeks,* and 'missy thang' is already out for some vernacular exercise?"

"Two weeks and three days," Vy asserts. "Almost four. And I'll give up 'missy thang' when you get rid of 'vernacular exercise.'"

Brooke, who has given us a backup soundtrack of soft giggles, suddenly sobers. "Sorry, M. I've let her slide a little. Things have been a little...strange around here lately."

"Strange?" I push aside a few of the dresses, needing to sit down. "That does not sound...good."

Understatement. All the strain I have sensed from them is not my imagination—and I shiver just from wondering why.

"Oh, *now* you have her going, Brooke."

"Have me going where?" I demand. "And why?"

"It's nothing." Brooke waves a hand in front of her awkward frown. "It's probably nothing."

"*Probably?*" My chest feels rubber-banded. "What does that—" I cannot finish. Coming from Brooke, who is married to the head of all Arcadian security forces, it could mean anything—but I force my mind away from the direst scenarios. The ones left behind are not the most comforting either. "Should Cassian be ordering the plane to take me home instead of sending me more dresses?" Because there *will* be more—of that, I have no doubt.

"All right. Hold on and chug a chill." Vy throws up a speak-to-the-hand too, with much more purpose than Brooke's fly swat. "The heightened security watches could just as well be practice drills, and—"

"Heightened security watches?" My optimistic resolve crumbles. My thoughts race, bringing up the period that changed so much for Arcadia three and a half months ago—thanks to the vigilante group who forced King Evrest to fake his own death, thrusting Samsyn onto the Arcadian throne. Thank the Creator, the movement was swiftly put down—though not the outside forces suspected of inspiring and funding it. "Are the...Pura...back?" I grimace, loathing even having to utter their name.

"No," Vy protests.

"We don't know," Brooke says at the same time.

"Saynt." His name shoots off my lips, an arrow off the bow of my fear. He is technically not a soldier yet, but desperate times beget desperate measures. Where is he, even now? It is a new day on the island. Is he getting ready for one of those watches? Surely he is not getting done with one. They would not place him on a dangerous night watch so soon. In so many ways, he is still just a boy...

"He's *fine*, girlfriend." Brooke's words are jabbed with conviction, confirming she has checked that veracity herself. "If anything, he's jonesing for action a little too hard for Samsyn's liking." She inhales with meaning. "But I know how the kid feels."

Slowly, a smile returns to my lips. I hope she can see the gratitude behind it. I miss my feisty former boss—even her daily grumblings about the grind of being a princess instead of a warrior.

"Well...keep him in line," I reply good-naturedly.

"We *both* are," Vy assures. "Just like his big sistah would."

"Speaking of keeping males in line..." Brooke exaggerates a brow waggle. "Can we get back to the subject—or should I say the confusing jerk—at hand?"

"And the fact that the blue gown will drive him more insane than the black?"

The dress Vy refers to, a sparkly pale-blue sheath, is nearly the color of my eyes—not that Cassian will notice my eyes with its plunging neckline. Brooke's top choice is a flowing black creation with an equally dramatic bodice: newly arrived from Milan, according to the curious little woman who has come every morning with fresh batches of gowns, per Cassian's directive—or so she tells me. The man himself has not given me more than twenty words since our "discussion" in the study last week, choosing to work late and eat elsewhere— sometimes even just spending the night at the office. I have little hope that this Literacy Ball is going to change anything but vow to give it a go.

And yes...perhaps there is a small part of me that wants to really be a princess for a night. Just this once...

"Show us both the dresses again." Brooke's request tugs my mind back to the present—away from its empathy with the sobbing sky outside. Like my spirit, the New York weather has been nonstop on the soggy for days. I welcome the chance to flip the smart pad screen, panning it across the bed. As I do, she emits a low whistle. "Daaammmn, girl. You know I'm not into apology by foof, but that man *is* trying to tell you something."

"Concurred." I change the screen back, to let them see my little shrug. "He is trying, I think...in his own weird way."

Brooke laughs. "What man *doesn't* have 'his own weird way'?"

"Mine," Vylet retorts. "What you see is what you get with Alak Navarre, thank the Creator. And for the record, I am keeping the hell out of him, so neither of you get any ideas."

I move to the window seat. Gaze over the labyrinth of wet streets below, the streetlights and neon signs blended by the rain into a giant watercolor. I would have much the same view from Turret One, which is one floor directly above—but I have not returned to that space, perhaps in subliminal protest to the continued lockdown of the other tower. As long as it stays shackled, I cannot help but feel a similar weight, invisible but just as formidable, on my spirit.

"Can you just lend Alak out for a while?" I venture. "How long do you think it would take for him to rub off on Cassian, just a little?"

Brooke sighs. "I think that lesson has to come from you, girlfriend."

Vylet smirks. "Which, coincidentally, might be best with a little...rubbing."

Brooke peels off a giggle. I groan. *Like old times.*

Perhaps too much.

I bite my lip. Too late. The backs of my eyes burn. "Creator's toes," I whisper. "I miss you both so much."

Stunningly, Vy is the first to sober on their end. Even more astonishing, her next words aren't *then just come home.* She gives four even better.

"We are already there."

As Brooke nods, her eyes are shiny too. "She's right, Shella-bean. We haven't gone far...the same way you aren't ever far from *us.*"

Now the rain falls inside too. I grip the smart pad as the flooding love of their friendship hits, a storm my heart has desperately needed. One awful sob overcomes another and another and another. They wait as only best friends can, their silence as perfect as a pair of hugs.

"I—I d-do not know wh-what—to do." The confession finally stutters out. "I—I feel so much for him..."

So much. The *new* understatement. But I am so afraid of saying more. Saying it will make it real. Too real. *And too much...*

"I told you, B," Vy murmurs after a pause. "Did I not?"

"Sure did," Brooke replies.

"T-Told her wh-what?" Despite the stammer, I sound shockingly pragmatic. At least I hope.

Vylet folds her arms, leans toward her camera, and nods with confidence. "That Cassian Court was going to be the man who changed you."

They both smile. I blush furiously. "Wh-When did you tell her that?"

"From the second he first took your hand, at that reception."

Brooke nods. "That *is* what she said."

Vy maintains her close-up angle. Studies me with the intensity only possible in her big movie star eyes. "Mishella—"

I get in my turn at hoisting a hand. "No. Do *not* ask it, Vylet Hester."

"—are you in love with him?"

Yes.

No!

"I—I do not know." I let out a new moan, conking my head back against the wall. "By the Creator. I am a mess..."

"That's all right." Brooke's interjection is as gentle as the rain against the glass. "Who said life is always neat and clean?"

"She did," Vy snorts.

After joining my watery laugh to theirs, I mutter, "Point made...dammit."

"Karma *is* a nasty bitch sometimes."

"No," Brooke interjects. "That little Prim what's-her-name. *She's* the bitch."

I shake my head—more violently than I can believe. "It is... bizarre...but I do not believe that. She *does* have a connection to Cassian—"

"You mean hooks?" Vy charges.

"Perhaps even that." My concession clearly spoils a little of her fun—the woman is always up for a rowdy debate—but I continue, "Though they are not romantic ones." I shrug, trying to sort through my bafflement. It is no use. "*Aggghh*. There are simply things I do not know." Rough breath in. Painful exhale. "Ghosts...he will not reveal."

Silence. Contemplative but not uncomfortable. Though they are half a world away, sitting with my thoughts is so much easier with the sis-friend-hood around.

At last, Brooke penetrates the pause. "Well, I understand ghosts," she offers quietly. "Samsyn carries a bunch. A real sucky hazard of the job."

I meet her gaze, which has turned as somber as the thunderheads outside. "But he tells you about them, right?"

"*Now* he does. But we're married, bean—and had six years of friendship before the rings went on our fingers. Things are very different for us."

"Of course." There is no use disguising my disappointment.

Brooke's lips flatten. I know the look but have never dreaded it as much as this moment. *Tough love.* "Mishella...the plan right now is that you're there for just six months. So now you have to ask yourself—is that a tolerable time to live with the ghosts?" Her shoulders rise and then fall. "I can't answer it for you, and neither can Vy."

I swallow deeply. "I just want him to be happy."

She sighs softly. "Perhaps that's your problem, girlfriend."

"Huh?"

"You *already* make him happy," she contends. "But maybe..."

"Maybe what?"

"Maybe you want something more than just that."

"*Just* that?" I openly glower. What is she talking about? Are there "levels" of happiness I do not know about, like they talk about on the cable service ads on the television? *Basic, deluxe, premium?*

"I'm just saying that maybe you crave...more." Her own face twists, as if a small skirmish is taking place in her head, before a heavy breath rushes out. "A more he's not capable of feeling or giving. Not right now."

Not to you.

I let the words—hers *and* mine—descend into taut silence. That is usually what people do when their heart is scooped out of their chest...yes?

"Mishella—"

"Fine." I abhor the terse snap but cannot help it from spilling. I cannot bear a moment of her getting apologetic about it—or, worse yet, pitying. "I—I understand, all right? And I am fine."

"All right, *stop*." Vy points a finger at her camera. "Do not punish Brooke for this. She is trying to help you see this clearly."

I force my lips into a girl Buddha smile. Do not let the serenity climb anywhere near my eyes. Continue to let them simmer while rejoining, "I see everything just fine, Vylet Hester. Now...I am certain both of you have a busy day ahead. I shall let you get to it."

I click my end of the call short without giving them a chance for farewells. It is a childish move—*I am taking my sand toys and going home*—but I cannot control the reflex any more than the frustration and fury spawning it. Both take over now, annihilating and untamed, and then dump out in an unhindered flood. A long, lonely, ugly cry in a room full of silk, satin, and brocade—finery I would trade in a moment for the true fullness of Cassian Court's heart.

CASSIAN

Holy fuck.

I must be dreaming.

"No shit," Scott mutters, confirming I've let the words slip aloud. Not surprising—nor would I be stunned if it happened again, as my Ella from the cinders seems to float down the steps, directing her soft smile toward where I wait by the car.

I'm not there for long—as in bolting to get the jump on Scott, who's done the "courtly" thing by stepping up to "collect" her for me—but I'm screwed for watching *any* man get near her tonight. Delaying the torture a little longer delivers a solid for all.

Annnd we can start with the solid any*time now...*

But fate is already having his fun with me tonight. The fucker takes his sweet time about the *kumbaya* with my nervous system, letting lightning raze me as she steps closer. The skirt of her gown, made of something that looks like a cloud spun into fabric, swirls and sparkles against the stairs with every step she takes. I pray for a breeze, which would likely flatten the filmy fabric around her thighs...

And just like that, *solid* arrives.

Between my legs.

Focusing on things above her waist is an only slightly better solution. The gown's strapless bodice is encrusted with gold and silver beads, with a band of the same defining the curve of her waist. While the neckline doesn't plunge that far down, thank God, the beads have been glued to lead one's eye toward the center—and the bit of her breasts that *are* revealed.

Too damn much for my liking.

Yet I can't stop staring.

Fuck. *Fuck.*

I had to go and hire the city's best hair and makeup to primp her too, didn't I? Damn that Fabiola, rubbing something into Ella's skin to turn it more enticing than it already is. The cream, or whatever the hell it is, gives her neck, shoulders, and arms some kind of iridescence...flooding me with visions of exploring all those planes with my tongue.

Not. Fucking. Helping.

My mind growls it out—like my body needs help remembering how long it's endured without hers. How many days we've wasted in this balance between the heaven of where we started and the hell we're most afraid of, both of us frozen on the tightrope, unwilling to move past the stupidity of surface niceties anymore. I haven't helped the situation by practically living at the office, but coming home to a place that really *is* temptation for me now, with her scent and her presence in every molecule of the air, has been a fiasco I made no plans for.

Plans.

*You actually started thinking of them in conjunction with this woman...*when?

Something will have to happen soon. I admit it now. She's not happy, and the sole plug she's given me back to her joy is not a circuit I can connect—not without frying every inch of my psyche. I know *that* now too, courtesy of the erotic memories that assault my mind's idle hours. Reliving every moment I've spent touching her, kissing her, fucking her, only clarifies the understanding. If she's capable of consuming that much of me sexually, how much more will she gouge from me emotionally?

There's no halfway with her.

Goddammit, there never will be.

Meaning I have to think about letting her leave.

"*Bon aksam*, Mr. Court."

Especially if she insists on issuing a lot more greetings like that. Professional cool backlit with sensual music, making me a new fan of the whole boss-and-secretary thing...

"And good evening to you, Miss Santelle."

And *especially* if I'll keep being required to bend over her hand like this—snapping a certain something beneath the tux like a goddamn ripe cucumber.

"Well." She yanks in a breath, lifting a shaky smile. I'll take it. After ten days of watching the dry cleaners' delivery guy get more friendly words than me, *I'll fucking take it.* "Here...we are."

Only by filling my lungs with air do I resist kissing away her nervousness. Instead, I go for a friendly smile and an overlay of charm. "It would appear so."

"That tuxedo is on the cutting edge of...something." She gestures with her free hand. "Fabiola told me. *Several* times."

I press in my lips, working the dimples. No way have I missed what their deployment usually does to her libido—and friendly or not, I'm still not above a few dirty tactics. "I'm sure she did."

She lowers her hand. Flits it at her skirt. "Well, you look very dashing."

"And you look like something I've only ever dreamed."

It wasn't what I'd planned to say—though that isn't astounding anymore, not when Ella's involved. And dammit,

I may be ready to *think* about letting her go, but I sure as hell haven't reached acceptance yet. Psychologically speaking, I'm in the "fight for it" phase.

I've fought for things a lot less important...

and won.

"Should we be off?" I murmur, tucking her hand beneath my elbow.

Her flits at the dress turn into full twists. "Sure. Um...I mean...certainly. Of course."

I mold my hand over the back of hers. "It's okay, Ella. I already know you're going to be the most beautiful one at the ball."

It's also what I'm afraid of.

She licks the seam of her lips, looking tempted to fully bite despite the contours of lip rouge representing at least thirty minutes of Fabiola's time. "I suppose I shall do," she finally mutters. "I mean...for the hired help."

I halt where I'm at. Slide my grip to her wrist and twist in—though now, we're close enough to the Jag that I have to let her go. She dives into the back seat like a pony let off its training harness—after a charming greeting and smile for Scott.

I remain rooted in place. Carefully reel back the ire that's just tumbled in with her. Tug hard at my jacket—and, with gritted teeth, order my cock to a stand-down too.

Fighting for this shit just got very serious.

Scott bounces on his toes, his normal puppy-bright self. "And good evening to you as well, Mr. Court. To the public library, right?"

"Not. Yet."

The puppy freezes. "Sir?"

I don't swerve my glare from its angle into the car—and

the lofty posture of the woman inside, thinking she's stilled me on the tightrope yet again. "Take the long way there," I command tightly. "A couple of times. No"—I stop, one hand on the open door—"just keep driving, until you hear from me."

Scott, not being stupid, raises the driver barrier the second he starts the car.

I'm not a stupid man either. As soon as we roll, I reach and brace Mishella by the hips. Haul her over from the spot beneath the opposite window until she's in the middle of the bench seat—right next to me.

"What on—"

"Be quiet, Ella." With a violent *thwick*, I pull a seat belt out. Snap it into the holster at her hip, securing her arm to her side in the doing.

"Cassian. *What* the hell are you—"

"I said be quiet." I let her glimpse my eyes, on fire with rage, while pressing her other arm to her side. "You'll have your chance to speak—momentarily."

Thwick.

Since the seat can accommodate three, one of the seat belts descends the opposite direction.

Clack.

I slam the buckle in, ensuring the straps are crisscrossed over her arms and torso. Now, the belts rise and fall with the frenetic pumps of her lungs. *Hell.* That neckline isn't as demure as I first thought. The sight of her breasts, creamy and gorgeous and just an inch from spilling full nipple, takes my cock to something between throbbing and unbearable. Not that I help matters by leaning over and clamping my hands over her wrists—but dammit, this shit has gone on long enough. If I'm going to be ordering up the plane to take her back to Arcadia tomorrow, she'll fucking hear out my side of all this first.

"I—I object to this!" Her eyes fire at me, bright as sun through blue glass. Her breasts show subtle pink strips from where they push at the straps. God*damn*. Why didn't I think of doing this a week ago?

"Are you in any physical pain?"

Her lips, already open to rage at me more, clamp shut. Pop back open to retort, "I—you're—"

"Hurting you?" I volley. "In *any* way at all?"

"Well...no. But—"

"Then you'll sit right here...and listen to me." I take in her open astonishment—and actually share some of it. My first sight of her full anger is more potent than I ever expected. She's an extra shot at last call. A hard bite into a jalapeño. A scoop of phaal curry. Intoxicating. Blistering. I want more and hate myself for it.

"*Listen* to you?" Her eyes narrow. "All I have *wanted* to do is listen to you, Cassian. I begged you to let me do just that—"

"When *you* were calling the subject matter." I constrict my grip. "Well, now I'm calling it. And the subject tonight...is you."

Her mouth opens again. Releases nothing but pissed-off little grunts, as her brain clearly struggles for a comeback. "There—there is nothing about *me* worth—"

"Oh no? Except the fact that you have labeled yourself everything from my fuck friend, my booty call, and now my hired help?"

I push deeper into her personal space, until my hips prod her knees apart and I breathe in her perfect scents. That exotic vanilla of her hair, its up-do layered with products from Fabiola's arsenal. Equally exclusive perfume—Chanel Grand

Extrait, Fab's favorite—jasmine and rose in a lush mix. The creamy luxury of whatever the hell makes her skin shimmer like this...and feel this damn good.

So. Damn. Good.

"Goddammit, Ella," I finally snarl. "You are *none* of those things. You never have been. How can you *think* them, let alone speak them?"

We both breathe harder. Our gazes meet and tangle. "Cassian." It's a sob, and I'm glad of it. I rejoice in her conflict. *Good. It's been hell for you too. I hope it's been* a lot *of hell.*

"Do you really think you're just a toy to me? A trinket I wanted and went after, like a car or a house or a suit?" I spit the final syllable, hating the raw emotion I swore not to expose—then even more for the surge of satisfaction as she flinches. "Did I experience something different, the moment our hands first touched...the second our eyes first locked?" I drill my stare harder into her. Slip my hands down until our fingers lace. "Was I the only one who thought the whole room had fallen away—hell, the whole damn island—until it was just you and me, standing on a rock in the middle of that ocean, put there by destiny?"

"No." As she rasps it, her fingers curl into mine. Her face lifts, eyes searching into mine. "No. You...were not...the only one."

More feelings hit. They're like waves in the sea I've just evoked: some fast and powerful and violent, some deep and rolling and continent-changing. I grit my teeth, willing them to get the hell over with things and drown me, but they're a storm surge, relentless against the ramparts of my spirit and soul. They tumble in, taking over my dark corners—the places I've vowed no one will get to, *ever* again. But here my Ella is, not just flooding them. She's changing them. Moving my continents...

"Then why?" I finally grate. "*Why* do you reduce it all to such ugliness? Why do you brand my heart with nothing but dollar signs—when I would have cut the fucker right out of my body and given it to your father, if that's what he demanded?" Maybe that would've been the better call anyway. Inside my chest or out, the thing is destined to beat on empty space without her. Maybe that's better, in the end—more bearable than the memories, the helplessness, the pain.

Her lips tremble. Her eyes shimmer. "Is that the key to knowing that heart, then?" A sound chokes from her throat, bitterness that doesn't make it to a laugh. "Because that is all *I* want, Cassian. Can *you* not see? The same way you have taken my heart, my *life*, and given them so much more meaning and worth...all I want to do is the same for you. To show you—"

"Show me *what*?" I release the burst without restraint or balance. *Isn't this what you want, Miss Santelle? Glorious, violent honesty? Fan-fucking-tastic. Let's do honest.* "You want to show that you can 'get' to me? That you can make me give you the 'ghosts,' so you can...what...exorcise them for me? That the power of your adoration is going to 'change' me? *Christ.*"

The last of it scorches my throat—burning past my crumbled resistance, overcoming the flood, eviscerating everything inside with its rage and shame and scorn. With a terrible growl, I let up on her arms. With another one, set her free from the seat belts. But the fire sweeps in, worse than before. It slams me to my haunches, coiling fists against my gut, fighting its incursion—and losing.

The car takes a corner. It's a gentle roll but, joined with the heat in my psyche, is enough to pitch me forward once more. My head swims, dizzy. My heart lurches, lost.

"C-Cassian?"

I watch my fist, clenched against the limo's gray carpet, vanish beneath the volumes of her skirt. Jerk it back, twisting it against the center of my chest. "Get away, Ella."

"No." Tears crack her voice, and I steel myself against them. Stiffen myself against the perfect warmth of her hands, pulling on the back of my neck, the whole of my scalp. "No. You do not want that." She draws me closer. Tighter into the embrace of her softness, her fragrance...her light.

It is time to live in the light...

Denial explodes from my soul. Churns in my chest. Snarls up my throat. "Leave. Me. Alone!"

Alone is the only place that makes sense.

Alone is the only place I won't hurt you.

The only place you *won't hurt* me.

But she pulls me harder—how the fuck did she get so strong?—and I'm letting her—how the fuck did I get so weak?—and her fingers dig into my face, forcing it up, commanding me to take in every breathtaking inch of hers. Yes, even the tears streaking it. Even the smudges of her lipstick, from where she's buried her face into my hair. But especially the glory of her eyes, adoring me...ambushing me...

"You are not alone."

Before she forces me closer and kisses me.

And kisses me.

And kisses me.

I am helpless against the magic of her lips. Consumed by the power of her embrace. Hardened by the nearness of her body.

Suffused by the force of her light.

"Fuck." It's helpless and guttural as she washes over me...

into me. *"Fuck."*

I lurch up, matching the force of her mouth with mine. Suck her in, feasting on the wet, warm depths that haven't been mine for so long. Too damn long...

Moans escape us. Our mouths reverberate with the sounds, inciting more heat through our limbs. Ella's hands cascade to my shoulders, finding their way beneath my jacket and then scratching at my shoulders through my shirt. I go at her with the same ferocity, wrapping one arm around her waist and sliding the opposite hand beneath her bodice.

"Oh!" It sparks off her lips, high-pitched and breathless, as soon as I find her first full nipple. I tease a finger across the tight peak. Then another.

"So hard," I utter against her lips. "So erect. So perfect."

She mewls as I glide my touch to the other. "They have been like this...all week."

"Really?"

She meets my frown with a kittenish smile. "Side effect of the injection. And being without you."

I lean in, kissing her deeply once more. "I've missed you too. Dammit, armeau...like missing my own legs. One day, I even forgot what day of the week it was—in the middle of a huge meeting, at that."

We laugh together. It feels so fucking good that I slide my eyes shut, savoring the emotional orgasm of the moment, praying the blinding blast of it lasts forever.

The glaring light of it...

I bolt from the recognition by losing myself in another kiss—and dragging her into its illicit darkness with me. Plunging the corners of her mouth with open, wicked, searing abandon, rolling our tongues until we both can't breathe and then pulling us both even deeper into the lusting, wild abyss...

Yes.

Yes.

This is what we need. If only for now, *this* is what we can claim as right between us. This is where I can give her exactly what she wants. I pull back, letting her see exactly that in my gaze, before spinning her around and making her face the seat. I tug at her arms, directing her to spread them out—and then press in and down, letting her feel every hard, lusting inch of my body.

I dip in, fitting my mouth against her neck. Snarl again, reveling in the hammer of her pulse under my lips.

"*Cassian.*" She battles to lift up, hitching her shoulders against my chest. Mewls with passionate force as I push her back down, skating my hands down her arms and twining my hands over the backs of hers. "Oh, please..."

"Please what, favori?" I softly bite her shoulder. "You want to keep talking about the light..." Another bite. Harder. "Or do you want a trip into the darkness?"

Her breath expels in a needy rush. "By the powers."

"That's not an answer."

"Take me...down," she finally pleads. "Into the...darkness. With you, Cassian. With *all* of you..."

As soon as the concession leaves her lips, I start shoving her skirts up. It takes a shorter time than I'd estimated to find her ass, barely sheathed in a thong surely mandated by Fabiola, but right now I'm certain I could locate this woman in another galaxy if forced to.

Appropriate imagery—since I damn near see stars the moment my fingers glide beneath those scant panties to the wet perfection between her legs. "And all of you too?" I work my fingers beyond her damp curls and then between her slick lips, stroking the inlet to her tunnel with the rhythmic touch that drives her crazy. In return, her thighs clench, her whole pussy shivers.

"Yes. Oh dear Creator; *yes*...with all of me!"

At first, I can only grunt. The heaven of touching her again, along with the hell of controlling my cock's reaction, are a purgatory too intense for words. My brain scrambles, trying to tell my body what to do. *Unlatch pants. Pull down zipper. Get yourself out of these fucking briefs.*

Another grunt, rapidly turned into a groan, as I lube myself with precome. Wildly unnecessary. "So wet," I growl, stating the obvious. "Christ, Ella. Your cunt is dripping."

She whimpers. "Take it. Take *me*. Into the dark. All the way. *Please*..."

I shove her panties farther aside. Notch my agonized crown against her tight cushions. "This isn't going to be gentle." It's not an apology.

"Thank the fucking Creator."

I lunge.

She screams.

We shake together, our bodies roaring in gratitude. I'm seated inside her, naked and pulsing, head to balls. *Fucking heaven.*

My forehead falls to her collarbone. My hands force hers outward, stretching her...until she's crushed against the seat beneath me.

I pull out. Nearly all the way.

Thrust in again, deeper than before.

Again.

Again.

Scott keeps driving. Around us, the city thrums with horns and hawkers, sirens and shouts, rock music and rowdy madness—but in here, in the haven of our darkness, there is only the wet rhythm of our bodies, the climbing force of our passion...the precipice to which we climb, aching to fall over together once again...

"Cassian. Oh...*my. Cassian!*"

"I know, sweet armeau. I know."

"So...close. I...am...*so* close."

"Widen your knees. It's going to spread everything for you."

I feel the exact moment she complies. Before she can even cry out, her walls clench in, surrounding me in the heated vise of her body. My dick answers with a swell of pressure, punching me deeper in, pulling me closer to the sublime end of my sanity. To make it better for us both, I add a subtle roll at the end of each thrust. If the seat is grinding her clit as I think it is, the effect on her arousal will be—

"Cassian! *Fuck!*"

Damn. *Damn.* That word, on her lips...even my hair follicles sizzle. I sink my teeth into her shoulder and don't relent one inch on driving hard into her sweet, tight body. "You like that, favori?"

"Uh," she gasps. "Uh-huh..."

"Of course you do. My perfect girl." I run my hands back up, cupping beneath her bodice. Pinch her nipples again, reveling in her throaty cry, before delving my hold back beneath the dress. My hands dive in, bracing her hips. My head fits against her neck. "My perfect girl, in the dark...where it's filthy and hot and my cock is buried so deep inside you..."

She inhales, shaky and edgy. Exhales between her teeth,

as her hands fist around the seat buckles. "Yes," she pants. "Yes. More. Take me there. *Take. Me. There.*"

And...that's it. Her plea snicks open the lock on my remaining restraint. With a punishing pace, I fuck her body back onto mine. I ram forward with the same force, feeding her the dialogue she craves with equally nasty intensity.

"The only place I'm taking you is under me, woman."

"Yes..."

"Taking my cock...bare...hard...deep."

"Yes!"

"Your cunt will keep taking it...and so will your clit." The tiny tremors of her nub, now flicked by my balls, have *not* escaped my attention.

"Yes, Cassian. *Yes.*"

"Without barriers this time."

"None!"

"Feel me filling you...invading you...making you hotter by the moment, until you think you can't stand it anymore, and—"

Her shriek finally breaks in. "I *cannot*! Creator help me— Cassian, *please*—I cannot take it anymore!"

CHAPTER ELEVEN

MISHELLA

"What?" His voice is rougher, harder, and more ruthless with lust than I have ever fathomed it could be. It terrifies me. It galvanizes me. "*What* can't you take anymore, Ella? Tell. Me."

And as he finishes it with a sharp smack to my bottom...it soaks me.

"W-Waiting," I finally stammer. "I cannot wait any longer!"

"For what?"

I should be wiser about this by now. Should have known he would get me to this precipice, only to make me beg for the final fall over the cliff.

Because he knows I will adore him for every moment of it.

I shove my mind through sexual smoke. Pull up the words he demands—the words I need—to take us both to the edge...

"I cannot wait..." I frantically lick my lips. "To come. For you. Around you, Cassian."

A sound chugs from his chest, full of sensual approval. I swear I am glowing from it, though instantly he is all animal impatience again, prompting, "And what else?"

"And...for you to come too," I rasp.

The husky approval again. Brighter glow.

"Like this?" he encourages. "With my bare cock in your cunt?"

Oh. My.

This. Man.

How does he *do* this? How does he know the exact angle for his mental scalpel, dipping it into the exact place in my psyche that holds my naughtiest triggers...my deepest arousals?

And right now, does that answer even matter?

"Yes." I shove my hips back, grinding in time to the raw pace he sets. "Yes, Cassian...with your naked cock inside me."

"Right here? Fucking you in my back seat?"

"Right here, Cassian. Right now. Here, in the back of your car."

"Spilling my hot, thick come inside you...as anyone on this street can hear you screaming because of it?"

I cut into his last word by embodying it. My climax rips straight from my fantasies and rampages my body, tearing a shriek from my throat and filling my sex with a storm. Within seconds, it spirals into a tempest. With a violent groan of his own, Cassian gives me the flood of his seed, relentless with his thrusts until we are both breathless, limp, and sated.

Slowly, he relents his grip on my hips. Though I melt forward a little, he follows me down. With his body still locked inside mine, he trails kisses down and then back up my shoulder. Continues around to the dip between my shoulder blades. His breaths are long and lingering, turning my perspiration into tiny shivers. When they trickle the length of my body, my walls clench around him once more.

"*Christ.*" He grits it before zigzagging the tip of a finger down my back, causing me to grip him harder. He reprises the word, harsher now.

I cannot help a little laugh. Add a saucy glance over my shoulder. "It is your own fault."

"Yeah? You may just make it my 'fault' again." His face, defined by taut arousal, is still an ideal pairing with his tuxedo. He was probably one of those children who play-acted James Bond for the martinis and the girls, not the bad guy butt kicking. "Holy *fuck*, woman. I'm half-hard again already." When I tighten all my muscles again, deliberately this time, he delivers a sound slap to the cheek that didn't get it the first time. I yelp. He purrs.

"You are a beast," I tease.

"A beast who has to make an appearance at this goddamn gala. So tell your sweet body to let me go...please."

With as much care as we can give my gown, we slide away from each other. "At least the ball is at the library," I offer while he scoops a towel from the limo's bar and helps clean me up. "I can sneak off and read while you hog-nog with your people."

"Hob-nob?" he prompts.

"Hm. That too."

"Well, there's only *one* 'knob' that concerns me." His face contorts as he wraps a second towel around his sex—which backs up his honesty with its beautiful, half-erect state. "And yes, it misses you already."

"Well, *I* miss *him*."

He stills, towel still on his groin. "Him?"

Quick shrug. "Well, of course. He is part of you, so..."

"So is it just 'him'?" His lips twist once more, as he tucks himself back in. "Or is there a proper name involved here? How about...Eugene? Or something more basic? Bill? Bob?"

I hold up both hands. Return with a chuckle, "All right, now. There *is* such a thing as carrying things too far."

"We just fucked like animals from the Upper West Side to SoHo. How far would you consider *too* far?"

I do not miss the tightened corners of his eyes, nor the tension now twining his tone. Perhaps he already feels the difference in the air between us...how I have stuffed away my heart the same way he has pushed down his penis. Clinical? Yes. But survivable? That is the more important yes. Nothing has proved that more clearly than what has just happened between us—a joining that blazed my heart and soul more thoroughly than his essence seared my sex—making it doubly necessary to re-shield them both.

Before he can take over any more of them...

Before they swell too huge, even for the shields.

I smooth my skirts. Pull some tissues from the built-in dispenser in the ledge behind the seat, dabbing at the lipstick that now must be all over my face. "I simply think that boundaries are a smart idea...in some circumstances."

Cassian stiffens. His gaze turns the shade *and* texture of jade. "In *what* circumstances?"

I draw in a breath. *You knew this might happen. Remember what you mentally rehearsed.*

I reset my shoulders. Force my stare to align with his. *Creator help me.* A little of my resolve weakens. His eyes are still jade—but now cut into battle daggers. Comprehension has started to seep in.

"In *this* circumstance," I state, folding calm hands around the tissues. "Everything you said earlier, Cassian...it is true, of course. We enjoy a good connection. A blend of chemistry that is...very nice, and—"

"Nice?" As his growl slams the air, his brows descend over his glare. "Fuck. Are you really doing this? *Nice?*"

I toss the tissues aside. Recollect myself. I have vowed to remain clear about this, even if he cannot view the situation accurately. Not if we are both to emerge from this arrangement as sane entities. "We...enjoy each other," I venture again. "In many ways."

He matches my determined inhalation. Wraps one hand around his knee, the other on the back of the seat. A posture of openness...

and challenge.

"Fair statement," he replies. "And in many ways, correct." His stare sobers. The car glides through a small dip and sways gently, becoming the expectant metronome to his follow-up. "But...?"

"But..." I fill my lungs again. "I cannot keep 'enjoying' them as thoroughly as I have been. This is for the best, Cassian. I truly believe it and need you to do so as well."

CASSIAN

I don't know whether to throw a punch through the back window or just throw up. Neither option is comforting. Both are confusing as fuck.

This isn't the first time I've heard those words from a woman. *If I had a dollar*, right? It's damn near the borderline of my norm. Cassian meets girl. Cassian screws girl. Cassian tells girl she gets the Court charm, the Cassian cock, and the designer-clad arm at a few parties. Even pillow talk is part of the package...perhaps a few jokes as bonus, if things are going well.

No hearts. No flowers. And goddammit, *no* life story sharing.

Which brings us, at some point, to here. A *here* I am just fine with. Perhaps, in many instances, am grateful for.

But this time, the confines of this car—of this fucking *life* and the price fate has demanded from me for it—render me nothing but gutted. Same effect, anyhow.

I grit my teeth, pumping air like a bull as bile hollows my belly and self-disgust dices my intestines. I combat both by focusing on the floor near her feet. Minutes ago, my knees were planted there in order to pleasure her. I'm not above dropping there again, if I have to beg her.

But I wonder if even that will make a difference.

Her regal strength, one of the qualities that blew me away when first meeting her, is now my worst enemy. It retaliates from the depths of her eyes, dark and serious as a graveyard before dawn. In short, her resolve looks pretty fucking set.

Dammit.

Dammit.

"All right." Concealing the gravel from it is as hopeless as hiding bird crap on this car. Poetic fit, since my psyche is about the same texture. "I'd ask you to define 'for the best,' but it looks like you've got that figured out too."

A heavy gulp moves down her throat. "I—I have to take care of my heart, Cassian." For the first time since our bodies broke apart, her voice shakes. "I have not even been here a month, and I already feel it..."

"You feel what, armeau?"

Her gaze flares into a glare. *Armeau.* I'm exploiting her hesitation, and we both know it.

"Disappearing."

Hell. Her tactic is worse than mine. Honesty—as only she can use it against me. Like a laser wielded by a master surgeon, aimed right at my ugliest tumors...my deepest fear.

A world without connection again.

A world without her again.

"It is disappearing, Cassian...into you." Her hands rise, covering her whole face. The tips of her fingers turn white as she shakes her head, fighting the very words she's just confessed. "But there is nothing there for it," she rasps. "Nothing...except..."

"Walls." I take the responsibility of it from her. Let the word weigh my shoulders instead, praying like hell that somehow it will...

what?

Change anything?

Because it doesn't change a fucking thing.

Her heart is still her heart—a gift too precious for my keeping.

And mine is still mine—a mess too morbid for her to handle. For *anyone* to handle. So many have tried—Kate, Prim, and the countless others who thought they had the "right key" to me—but the truth is, only one person has even gotten close to that entrance. To breaking me open.

Shattering me whole.

And like an idiot, I reach again for her now.

I thank God—and any other entity who cares to take credit—when she lets me pull her closer, fitting her cheek atop my heart, spreading her warmth over my whole body. And yes, enticing the twitch parade to carry on in my dick—though that need comes a very distant second to getting an answer to the question on my lips now.

"So...what happens now, Ella?"

She shifts, nuzzling closer. *Good sign?*

"Are you asking if I want to go home?"

Bad sign.

"Yeah." I practically choke on the syllable. "Yeah, I guess that's what I *am* asking."

I remember something about her taking special courses on Arcadia, about courtly arts and practices. Undoubtedly, the fine skill of torture was in that mix. Her silence is nothing less.

"I do not want to go home, Cassian."

I breathe in, claiming back the year she's just stripped out of me. "Thank you." It needs to be said. Perhaps more than once. Maybe from that position I was contemplating, at her feet.

"But I need to move into one of the guest rooms."

"Sure." It spews too quickly and too eagerly, and I don't give a flying shit. I make a mental note to text Hodge and direct him to clutter up the two guest rooms farthest from the master, forcing her into the third. "Yeah. Okay."

"And we make dates to see each other," she goes on. "Real ones, where we go out in public and I get to meet your friends. What?" She knuckles me curiously in the ribs, responding to my snort. "You *do* have friends?"

"I suppose." I don't have the heart to tell her my closest "buddy" is Doyle, whose idea of stimulating conversation is four grunts, two beers, and a good Knicks game.

"Well, we can start with Kate. Is she dating anyone?"

"I don't know." That is usually the case—which, for the first time, comes as truly troubling.

"We can figure it out." The woman in my arms shifts back to central focus. I curl in my fingers, making light circles on her creamy shoulder, enjoying the musical cadence of her voice... rejoicing in the fact that it's not leaving me anytime soon. "The important thing is, we get *away* from Temptation so we are not always...well...*tempted.*"

Light chuckle. A gentle kiss into her hair. "Why, Miss Santelle, whatever do you mean?"

"Says the man with a woodshed poking my thigh?"

I laugh harder. *Much* harder. "You mean some wood?"

"Hm. That too."

CHAPTER TWELVE

MISHELLA

"Mishella?"

I hear Scott's concerned prompt, backed by the rush of traffic along 5th Avenue behind us, but cannot answer. My jaw has dropped on one of the most stunned gapes of my life.

"Armeau?" Cassian now, his body large and close, one hand curving around my elbow, his cedar scent a perfect blend with the grass, trees, and spring flowers abounding through Bryant Park. I now remember Brooke gushing about this place, once she learned that the Literacy Ball would be held at the big library here. Before her family went into hiding on Arcadia, when she was just a young senator's daughter, she attended something called Fashion Week. The event was a bore, she claimed, but the magnificence of Bryant Park was a win.

Now I understand why.

"Ella."

The urgency in his voice finally causes me to turn. I do not hide my continuing shock—as if that is even possible. "Cassian..."

His mouth hitches up at one end. "What, beautiful?"

"We are in the wrong place." I blurt it despite the small throng of other partygoers, strolling along the wide pathways and majestic steps of the soaring Beaux-Arts building before us.

Scott steps forward, darting a worried look. "This thing *is* at the library?" he queries Cassian. "Right?"

"But this is not a library."

"Huh?"

"It is a palace!"

Though Scott relaxes, his posture takes on a shrug. "No better place for books then, yeah?"

I absorb that with a wider smile. "Cassian?"

"Yes, armeau?"

"Give Scott a raise."

The young man breaks into a chuckle. "I think I'm going to like having her around, Mr. Court."

Cassian loops an arm around my waist, tugging me tightly. "Me too, Scott. Me too."

The Schwarzman building is more breathtaking on the inside. We enter Astor Hall by descending wide stone steps flanked by balustrades worthy of a Parisian palace, their fancy scrolls and swirls matching archways down the length of the room, all supporting a soaring, ornate ceiling. Similar carvings adorn the stone bases of multiple candelabra, all at least twenty feet high, lending a romantic glow along with colored lighting, purple and orange and amber, around the room's perimeter. From some hidden location, a string ensemble plays classic pieces.

I pull Cassian to a stop at the top of the stairs. Drag in a long breath, celebrating the very best aspect of the place.

"Books." I close my eyes, letting the glorious scent fill me. His guttural growl brings me back to attention. "What?" I add a perplexed giggle. It turns into a sigh when he lifts a grin, dimples on full display.

"Just ignore me." He leans closer, gaze hooded. "I was pretending the smell of three and a half million books really just hit you like an aphrodisiac."

I slink my regard to his mouth. It's one of the most fascinating parts of him, curving in new ways with all his moods. Aroused is definitely one of my favorites. "Maybe...it did." I slide a finger up his satin lapel. "Add some chocolate, and you may get lucky in the library, Cassian Court."

New growl. "I thought we were 'scheduling' dates now."

"Chocolate gets you priority status on the calendar."

His eyes darken to my favorite color—sage smoke—as he dips in, brushing those captivating lips to mine. "Before we sprint to the dessert buffet, I need to make a mental note."

"About what?"

"About buying a chocolate factory."

My giggle expands to a laugh, opening me for his full plunder. I am secretly—perhaps not-so-secretly—delighted when he does just that. Though we do not give in to a full "mack session," in Vy's terms, it is enough of a tangle to reheat my body's need for him—and rekindle my heart's hope that one day, he will think about trusting me with more than just his playful side.

"Well, Cassian Court! *There* you are!"

The exclamation, bursting the air like a full flock of geese, breaks us apart with matching effect. I look up, stunned to realize the voice belongs to a woman who appears more like a swan. Her steps are fluid glides, her arms float like a ballerina's, and her eyes are huge and dark against practically translucent skin.

"Carol Idelle." Cassian transforms back into a gallant

courtier, stepping forward and bowing low. The woman laughs, a new honk on the air, while tugging him close for air kisses. "Yes. Here I am."

Carol bats her eyes, making her false lashes look like swan wings in flight. The impression cannot be helped, since the lengths are a curious blend of black and white strands—but when the woman notices my gawk, she exaggerates the effect by tossing me a saucy wink.

I believe I like her.

"Well, better late than never—especially in your case, darling. You look a-maz-ing. Who did this for you? Tom Ford?"

"Valentino."

She huffs, accenting with a honk. "Of course. I was just speaking with Yolanda Wood. She guessed you'd pick Valentino. I was hoping for Ford."

Cassian's responding smile is, for a long moment, mesmerizing. I have not seen the expression for two weeks, since becoming obsessed with it from across the room at official Sancti court events. It is one part charm, one part decorum, one hundred percent sexy. From his first night on Arcadia, Vy nicknamed it "The Panty Melter." Watching Carol Idelle react to it now, I send a long-distance fist bump to my friend. *Right on the money, Vy.*

The reminiscence of my friend brings a shot of confidence at the perfect moment—for the woman decides to ogle *me* now. "And who is *this*...exquisite...creature?"

She draws out "exquisite" in a way that makes me doubt her sincerity. Glancing to Cassian for clarification lends no help. The Panty Melter remains across his lips, but the warmth is miles from reaching his eyes, even as he curves a hand around my waist again.

"I'm honored to introduce Mishella Santelle, gracing us with her presence from the Court of Arcadia. Ella, this is Dame Carol Idelle, a bastion of the city's library foundation, among other worthy endeavors."

I dip my head, offer my hand, and debate a curtsy. In the end, I simply murmur, "Bon aksam. It is lovely to make your acquaintance, Dame Idelle."

I refrain—barely—from starting when the woman releases her largest honk of all. Since the sound could be anything from a climax to a sneeze, I am not sure about selecting any other reaction.

Finally, she exclaims, "Oh, my *word*. Cassian, she is a-*dor*-a-ble. It is lovely to make *your* acquaintance as well, Mishella."

I open my mouth, preparing a proper return in the form of asking about the building's grand architecture—but the air is sliced by a new interruption.

No. Not sliced.

Butchered.

"*Lovely.*"

The word hacks at us, a mixture of drawl and shout that is so unmistakable, I can think of at least three Vy-isms to fit the mahogany brunette in the Romanesque red sheath, approaching on slinky steps with her clutch in one hand and martini glass in the other.

Tanked.

Shitfaced.

Annihilated.

But none of the labels matter the moment Cassian gives her just one.

"Amelie."

My heart tumbles into my stomach. Plummets even

further, sinking until my knees are weighted with the burden, and I grip Cassian for purchase. I have no doubts about getting it. Beneath my hold, his arm is a log of tension—a limb extended from the taut tree of his whole body.

Yolanda Wood at the Literacy Guild will need to be called. Clarify my RSVP is for two...my guest's name will definitely not be Amelie Hampton's.

"Well look who's here!" Carol saves us all from a honk—thank the Creator—with a cheerful clap. "Amelie, my dear. Don't you look stunning? Is that Christian Siriano?"

"Valentino." Amelie's button nose quirks with a strange expression, something between a huff and a flare. "I picked it tah match mah date." New nostril twitch. At some point in her life, someone probably told her the expression was cute. It is *not* cute—but it is also impossible for me to accept it for what it is: a drunk girl's dig at the man she wants to keep her claws embedded into. My heart continues racing through my body. My belly lurches, trying to keep up with the pace.

"Isn't *that* a coincidence," Carol croons. "Cassian is also—" She stops herself with a comprehending honk. "Oh. Oh, *dear.*"

Cassian, confirming he truly must have been James Bond in another life, dips a nod as if Amelie's glare is made of silk instead of mud. "You always *have* been the go-getter, Amelie. But it's always best to make sure the parachute's strapped on before you leap from the plane."

"Ha!" Carol claps again. "Isn't *that* just the way of it? Ohhh Cassian, you're a clever fellow by half."

Amelie sips at what is left of her drink. Bursts with a brittle laugh. "Isn't he *just*? Carol, ya make the most *astute* obsahvations." Another laugh gurgles out her nose. "Ya gettit? Asssss-tute. Asssss-tute. Hee hee."

Carol huffs. "It might be time to call a car for you, young lady."

Amelie hurls her a glare. "Ah'm *fine.*" Pulls back her shoulders so hard, her balance is thrown off. She wobbles. Drops her clutch. I hasten to help but am shoved away. "I said ah'm fine! Don't you *dare* touch my things, bitch!"

"*Amelie.*" Cassian steadies me with both hands, his grip as forceful as his voice. "*Enough.*"

"I am all right." I address the question in his gaze before he even utters it.

"I am all right." Surprisingly, her sing-song echo does not change my stance—perhaps because I know it for the imbecile move that it is. Even so, the poor woman does not know the difference. "I am all right, Cassian. Jush because you're here now, Cassian. Oh, hold muh now, Cassian. Ah love you, Cassian!"

By the powers. Could she dig her grave any deeper?

"Amelie." Cassian is not a tree anymore. His frame is now a monolith of rancor, pushing the confines of his clothes. His hands tremor against my arms, betraying his battle for composure. "You. Are. *Done.*"

She spurts a high-pitched laugh. "Oh God, Cassian. I've known that for weeks now. But does *she*?" One whip of motion in my direction, and the woman has surrendered her martini to the center of my chest.

"Saint George on gingerbread," Carol mutters.

Cassian wheels away from me—straight at her. "Are you out of your goddamn mind?"

"No." She plants an action hero stance—stunning, given her gown *and* condition—and flings up an arm, cocktail glass still in hand. "But it's clear *you* are."

Before I can blink in comprehension, the glass has left her hand—cracking against Cassian's forehead before smashing to the floor.

"By the Creator!" I rush to him as Carol shouts for security.

Amelie struggles against the two officers who arrive, though the stare she swerves toward me, filled with she-cat celebration, is the first thing to truly scare me about the woman since she arrived. "Gah 'head, sugar plum," she purrs. "He's all yours now. Take gooood care of him, because ya won't get a chance at it for long."

Carol marches forward. Blasts at the guards, "Get her *out* of here!"

But their persistent prisoner breaks free. "Ya haven't told her yet—have ya, Cassian?" She cackles through a laugh as they wrestle her in again. "Ha! Imagine *that*. Cassian Court, preachin' about a girl bein' readah with the parachute—only *he's* holdin' the rip cord." Her head lolls to the side. "Or was it Lily who had the cord...in the end?"

I finally fish a tissue out of my purse—but as I raise it to Cassian's face, my hand trembles. The crowd that's gathered... they are surely here to watch the rambling soused girl, not her hapless target...

Then why do I feel the weight of a hundred stares on *my* back? Squirm against the potent heft of their curiosity and shock?

Feel the probe of Cassian's desperation because of it, even before he looks up, through his own blood, at me?

"Don't listen to her, Ella. *Don't. Listen.*"

I feel my stare narrow—as my heartbeat quickens. "Is there something to listen to?" A boulder careens down my throat when he gives back only thick silence. *"Cassian?"*

"Ohhhh, wait. Maybuh she's jusss your type, Cas. Sweet. Cute. Clingy. Suicidal. Right?"

"Fuck." Cassian mutters it...as the tissue drops from my limp fingers.

"What'd'ya think, little Arcadian princess? Ya have what it takes to be a real Lily Rianna Court, hmmm?"

Her giggle blends with the crowd's buzz, rising with the pitch only possible with a mix of nerves and scandal—a sound with which I am sadly familiar, thanks to the machinations of the Sancti Court.

As the guards jostle her out the door, Amelie starts to sing, high-pitched and off-key. "Lileee of the vallleee...you are so beeeaut-i-fulll to meee..."

In the strange hush that follows, my lungs fight for air.

The crowd still gawks.

As the whispers begin.

And the walls close in. And the room becomes my prison.

"Ella?"

And his voice, my cruel jailer.

"Ella?"

I take jerking steps back. Hold out my hands at his face, now wavering in the blur of my tears. "I—I need air. I have to get air."

"Ella!"

I do not listen. I do not turn. I cannot.

Somehow, I find my way back outside. It is not the same way we entered the building. Nothing is as bright here, and I am grateful for the shadowed paths. They...fit. More than I want to comprehend...

The only thing I can think about now.

Ella...it's time to live in the light.

"Bull...shit." It stutters out between sobs. Ends in a rasp, mingling with the streams down my face, that are finally rescued by gravity to fall away...

into the dark.

"Ella."

His voice makes me falter.

Fool. Fool.

I double my pace.

"Ella, for fuck's sake!"

I stop, telling myself it is more for me than him—that it has nothing to do with the serration in his voice or how his breath clutches at the end. I freeze, staring across the dark expanse of the park's main lawn. In the distance, *le carrousel* glows, alight but empty, only a promise of magic.

Like the man who scrambles to stand in front of me now.

"Ella."

"*No.*" It hurtles out, unthinking and unmitigated, from the same awful place where my tears live. My *fears*. The dread with which I have wrestled since the day I went to Kate's and learned that the knight who carried me off to his kingdom is not the shining Lancelot I originally painted into my Cassian Court journal...the omen that his "ghosts" were much more than just that and I would confront those specters too damn late?

After too much of my heart belonged to him.

Like now.

After the point of no return, between it hurting me...and crushing me.

Like now.

"No, Cassian. I—I cannot—"

"Or you will not?"

Again without thought, I whirl. Launch myself at him. "How dare you." Drive fists into his chest with any shred of strength I have left. "How *fucking* dare you." Pummel him again and again, until the tears build and swell and spill once more. "*I will not?* I will not *what*, Cassian? Hear *your* side now, after I begged you for it at Temptation? Try to make *sense* of you now? Try to figure out why you have crooned to me about our destiny, our connection, and our light, only to learn—in front of hundreds of people—that you were...that...you have... been..."

It grinds to a halt deep in my belly. Stuck in my soul. Brimming instead in my tears.

He speaks it instead.

With his tears soaking through it.

"Married."

I hate myself for gazing back to him. Hate myself even more for how my heart bursts once more for him, sprouting a million vines that reach for the brilliant sustenance of him... even now, as he falls to the grass in his darkest grief.

No.

Especially now.

Slowly, quietly, I lower next to him. As my skirt floats atop the grass, his hand folds over mine. Grips me with fervent force.

I hold on in return. Just as tight.

Finally, his voice quivers the air between us. "We were together...for a year. Married...for most of the next."

"Until she took her life." When he only nods, I go on. "And you...loved her?"

I pray he is not insulted by the query. It feels important for me to know...for absolute certain. Aside from Brooke and

Samsyn, and soon Evrest and Camellia, I do not know a single marriage born from love.

"Yes," he utters. "I loved her."

"But...?" It is as heavy in his tone as the dew across the grass.

"But it was a young love." He lifts his head. The wind loosens his hair, tumbling it into his eyes, which are earnest... and honest. "A boy's, for a girl. Not a man's...for a woman." His fingers twist tighter into mine. "Mishella..."

He pauses, giving me time to swallow. To breathe. To think.

Then to yank free from him.

To bolt to my feet. And turn. And run.

I refuse to let him speak it. I possess no doubt that he *means* it. But accepting it now, as some kind of enchanted glue to "fix" tonight—

No.

Not here, in our dark. In our rawness and weakness.

I need time. I am still...

afraid.

"Heyyyy. What is *such* a pretty lady doing, running around in the darkness like this?"

The voice clutches me to a new stop. My head jerks up, and my stare circles around. Lost in my emotions, I have stumbled all the way to the other side of the lawn—to the darker side of the park.

The much darker side.

Into a triangle of men who are definitely *not* attending the Literacy Ball.

Their faces are unshaven, though their heads are shiny and bald. Piercings turn the three of them into walking jewelr counters. More silver gleams from their fingers—and from the smirk I get from the one now blocking my path.

"I...umm...I apologize, gentlemen. I seem to have gotten a little turned around."

"Ohhhh." Another one sidles in from the left. "Did you hear that, guys? We're *gentlemen* now."

"Moron." The first one snorts. "We always *have* been gentlemen." His pierced brows waggle. "We just...got a little turned around too."

The third thug steps in from the right. "Maybe we can all get back on the 'straight and narrow' together."

I may be from an island not much larger than this one— and have not seen any of the world beyond it before two weeks ago.

Some may even call me naïve.

But I am not stupid.

I know when to scream as if my life is depending on it.

Because it is.

The world cartwheels and tilts. I kick and struggle, but they are strong and many—and the bushes into which they drag me are thick and twisted. And dark. *By the Creator*, so dark...

Somehow, I get my teeth into the grimy hand that's been clamped over my mouth.

"Dammit! *Bitch!*"

For a blessed moment, I am able to breathe again. And scream again. "*Help!* Somebod—"

"Shut her *up!*"

"And hold her down, dammit!"

A new hand clamps my mouth. More hands pin me down in a pile of leaves and dirt. Still, I never stop struggling, even as they shove my skirts to my waist. I never stop resisting, even as they grab at my thighs, and—

"Get. Your. Fucking. Hands. *Off of her.*"

Like a bullet shot into a flock of birds, the thugs jump up. I scramble backward, ignoring the twigs and thorns scratching me everywhere, unwilling to trust my trembling knees enough to stand. Fear seizes me like ice. Panic battles it, searing and dizzying. Nausea bubbles in my throat. "C-Cassian?" I finally get out in a choke.

"I'm not alone." It is him but not him. Rage is a living thing in his voice, a walking beast in his steps. "NYPD's two blocks away, and they've got a GPS lock on my cell."

"Let's beat it!"

"Come on, dickwad! Now!"

The new Cassian creature snarls again—and right now, it is the most wonderful sound in the world. "Listen to your pals, *dickwad.*"

I blink, battling to focus on him. Wonderful or not, he has confronted these monsters head on. I plead the thug with every exigency in my heart. *Please be a good dickwad and go away. Just go away!*

Creator's mercy. There is so much movement. So many shadows. It is all happening so fast...

"You know what, fancy ass? *Fuck you.*"

Then entirely too slow.

And with the cruel joke of horror, I can see him again.

As three bursts of light flare in the night.

And three bullets rip into the man I love.

CASSIAN

Way to fuck up a night, asshole.

At least I think it's still night. Police sirens sound diff

in the city at night. More desperate. And isn't that the moon, over the buildings, floating in the stars? It's right there. So beautiful. So unreachable.

'Cause you're a sky; 'cause you're a sky full of stars...

So cold.

Like me. Why the hell am I so cold? It's the end of May in New York City. I'm still in New York, right? At the Literacy Ball...kissing the woman I love.

No.

Chasing the woman I love.

I'm gonna give you my heart...

"Ella?"

"Cassian!"

"Ella." Why can't I reach her? Why can't I *move*? "Fuck. Ella."

"Do not move!"

"Okay."

"Help is coming!"

"Help for...what?"

"Sssshh. Save your strength. Be *still*, for Creator's sake!"

"Sssshh." I hurl it back defiantly. Reach up, needing to brush her tears back. Why is she still crying? All I've done tonight is make her cry. "It'll be all right. Everything will be all right."

Her shoulders shake. The cream curves of them are so perfect against the stars. Satin and light...my warmth in the chill. "Ridiculous man." Her watery smile beams into me. *All* of me. The soul I can no longer hide from her... "That is supposed to be my line."

"Why?"

Her head snaps up. The rest of her follows, scattering

leaves—*leaves?*—before she's gone and I'm cold again. So fucking cold.

Go on and tear me apart...

"Over here!" Her shout is shrill and scared. No. Terrified. "He is over here! Please...hurry!"

Why is she so frightened?

"Ella." It resonates in my head but is just a puff on my lips. *Ella. Come back. Please...*

"Help him. Please help him!"

"We will—but miss, in order for that to happen, you need to stand back."

"Cassian. I'm still here. I'm right here. Cassian...please hang on!"

I blink, forcing my head to twist, following the call of her voice. Focusing on her. Only on her...even as the cold closes in, gripping more of me than before...

'Cause you get lighter the more it gets dark...

CHAPTER THIRTEEN

MISHELLA

"Are you out of your fucking mind?"

Answering my brother's snarl with a manic giggle, even from thousands of miles away, does not feel like a good idea. He sounds like a completely different person. A forceful man has taken the place of my sweet little Saynt. How can so much have changed in just two weeks?

All too easily, my heart answers that one.

Two weeks can change everything.

One *night* can change everything.

I drag my head up. Force myself to gaze at my weary reflection in the window of the hospital's hallway. Beneath the denim jacket Prim offered from her own back after she and Hodge arrived, my gown is torn and dirty. I behold each smudge proudly. I am not the same person who first climbed into this dress.

I am a survivor.

I have earned the full right to laugh in my brother's face.

"I shall accept that as a supreme compliment, brother mine. And the short answer is: *yes*, I probably *am* out of my ʼʌcking mind. And proud *of* it."

Saynt huffs more heavily. "Mishella, you were assaulted—"

"Because I wandered somewhere I was not supposed to

be, in the middle of the night."

"—by *three* men—"

"And Brooke was taken captive by twice that many, less than a mile from the Sancti Palais."

"—in a city full of savages!"

"*Saynt.*" My laughter vanishes. "That. Is. Enough."

Moody silence. Then another guttural growl. "I told Court that if *anything* happened to you...if one *hair* on your head was hurt—"

"Enough!"

His answering breath is so rough, static invades the line. "Mishella...*please*," he finally grates. "Come home, where I can protect you."

I sigh but with conviction to match his. "Do Paipanne and Maimanne know you are asking this?"

"Do *you* know how unfair that question is?"

I give a mixture of grunt and hum, our sibling shorthand for an apology. He is right. My brief call with our parents, just thirty minutes ago, yielded their subdued concern—mostly about whether Cassian would hold his "misfortune" against me or not—but little else. If the decision is solely theirs, I am definitely staying in New York.

As Vy would say: *oh, the glorious irony.* For the first time in a long time, I want exactly what Mother and Father do.

"But what *you* are asking is equally unfair, Saynt Austyn Santelle." I let the rebuke set in before softly going on. "I know it sounds strange, even unbelievable, after what has happened... but please, *please* try to understand. I...belong here now, Saynt. In New York. With Cassian."

"Because you signed that fucking contract?"

"Because I have fallen in love with him."

And it took nearly losing him to realize it.

Another long silence.

As I have expected.

Saynt emerges from the shock with a few sputters—and I brace myself for the string of questions to come after *that*—but Cassian's nurse sprints into his room, clawing me with new dread from head to toe. Past the exposed nerves in its wake, I blurt a promise to Saynt that I shall call back and race in behind her.

"What is it? What is wrong? Is he—"

"Being completely difficult?" The nurse spits it over her shoulder, fighting Cassian for control of his oxygen mask.

"Oh." My fingers press my laughing lips. Surely I have earned a spot on the woman's "shit list" because of it, but holding back my exhilaration is a physical and emotional impossibility.

Ridiculous, tenacious, wonderfully *alive* man.

My man.

"This is New York Presbyterian, *not* Court Tower, mister." The nurse forces the plastic dome back over his nose and mouth. "You've just had three bullets pulled out of your body, which means *I'm* the boss for a while—and the boss says this stays on until your oxygen levels are better."

To my wonder—and, it seems, to hers—Cassian sinks back to the pillow. Gives a terse nod. She returns the action, looking satisfied with his sincerity.

I bite my lip.

I know better.

Sure enough, as soon as her footsteps fade down the hall, he shoves the mask away. His other hand is already full of mine, dragging me as close as his wounds will allow. Not being his immediate family, I have only been given generalities for updates. By the grace of the Creator, the punk in the park was a lousy shot, and none of the bullets hit major organs. The trauma surgery went well—and one look at the magnificence of Cassian Court's body, even encased in a hospital gown, is testament to his outstanding base health.

Still, the intensity of his grip is enough to pop my stare wide. "*Cassian.*" I almost add a maternal cluck, despite the *non*maternal thoughts inspired simply by his exposed knees. "Save your strength. The nurse is right. Your levels—"

"Will be fine." His throat sounds coated in twelve layers of rust—though after one second of his gaze, it is clear some are not physically related. "I have my air again."

Oh.

Him.

I lift the union of our hands. Several tubes take up the space on the back of his, so I turn it over and then press a kiss into his palm. "And I have mine."

His beautiful lips push together. He swallows heavily. "My mother—"

"Has been called," I assure. "Hodge handled it. He and Prim are downstairs, waiting for her." I crunch a little frown. "For some reason, *he* was listed as your emergency contact."

"Yeah." He nods before closing his eyes for a moment. "He can break things to her better than emergency personnel."

My frown deepens. "Has he had to do this before?"

He lets that fall into a long silence. Keeps his eyes closed the whole time. When he finally looks back up at me, it is with his lagoon-dark eyes—and his not-to-be-brooked intent. "I was awake...for a little while...before you came in. I heard you on the phone...with Saynt."

His allusion rests between us like a wick just catching fire—beautiful but uncertain. At last I whisper back, "Oh you did, did you?"

His hand lifts. Frames my face. "Did you mean it? Have you fallen in love with me, Ella...despite the secrets, the ghosts, the flying martini glasses, the New York City wildlife..."

I lean over...unable to hold back from sealing my mouth to his now. And yes, even here and even now, I am shocked we do not make the building's lights flicker with the flare of our attraction. Before his monitors dance too crazily, I pull away—if only by a few inches.

"Living in the wild is just perfect for me, Mr. Court...as long as I live in it with you."

CASSIAN

Nurse Ratchet is going to have to deal.

Kissing my woman again isn't negotiable.

Of course...this is more than a kiss.

It's a seal. The signet of my spirit, my soul, my heart...

Everything she has given back to me.

Everything I thought I'd never have again.

Everything that was robbed from me because of pain and loss and fear, instead of hope and belief and light.

And love.

Yeah...that.

I curl fingers into her hair. Pull her down a little more.

"I'm in love with you too." As a smile brims her lips and tears edge her eyes, I quickly clarify, "But favori, I'm rusty at this shit. *Really* rusty. I'm...I'm not going to get everything right."

She caresses through the stubble along my jaw. "And *that* is a news flush?"

"Well. It might be a news *flash* to some—but if you're patient, I promise...I'm a fast learner. It'll get better."

Fuck. So much better. My little sorceress probably doesn't realize it, but she's just dangled the biggest carrot for recuperating I could ever have. Dammit, I *will* get my ass out of this bed--and then get cracking on making every one of her dreams come true. There's an action item list well underway...

One: make love to her for a week straight.

Two: take her to Turret Two—and include *all* the details this time.

Three: make love to her for another week straight.

Four: bid on chocolate factories—preferably near libraries.

Five: take her to the newly purchased factory. Collect on preferred calendar status for date night.

"*Cassian.*" Her sweet, high sigh refocuses me on the here and now—and the temptation of her full lips, now parted in perfect invitation. I lift up...and sweep in. She moans, sighing again. I steal her breath and give her back my own.

My air...

Our tongues tangle. Taste. Conquer. Surrender.

My love...

But the completion of the moment...is the beating of her heart. Pressed to mine, matching mine...knowing mine so far beyond the flimsy confines of the time we've had physically together. She knows me from the depths of fate—from the forever of the destiny that has completely, absolutely, brough us together. The destiny I'm trusting again now...no matt how fucking terrified I am.

But I refuse to live in that fear.

Once more, despite the fear raiding every cell of my body because of it, I choose love.

I choose her.

I'm opening the gift.

Continue the Temptation Court Series with Book Two

Pretty Perfect Toy

Keep reading for an excerpt!

EXCERPT FROM *PRETTY PERFECT TOY*

BOOK TWO IN THE TEMPTATION COURT SERIES

MISHELLA

I am going to hell.

A choir sings in Latin. People speak in reverent tones. Sun streams through angels and saints on stained-glass windows, dappling rainbows across pious stone effigies...

And all I can think about is undressing the golden perfection of a man next to me.

And that would only be the start.

I want to touch him. Caress every muscled, chiseled inch of him. Wrap my naked body around his. Guide his erect, straining body deep inside mine...

Not. Now.

But why not now?

Cassian. I ache...

Nearly six weeks have passed since the moment that changed our lives. Forty-one days, to be exact—since the night he confronted a group of hoodlums attacking me in a dark corner of Bryant Park, not knowing one of them was carrying a gun—that the thug then fired three times.

Even here, in the streaming sun of mid-July, I relive that horrific midnight as if it has just happened. The minutes, seeming like hours, of gripping his pale hand, locking my terrified gaze into his glassy one, screaming across the park for help until I was hoarse...and then screaming some more...

"Please! Come quickly! His name is Cassian Court. Yes, that Cassian Court. You must help him! You must—"

"Ella."

My head snaps up. He is not pale any longer, thank the Creator—a little patch on his elegant nose actually peels from the sunburn he incurred during our sailing trip on New York Harbor over the weekend—and his eyes are glittering instead of glassy, as deep a forest green as the T-shirt hugging his flawless torso. Regrettably, *that* is mostly hidden now, layered beneath a tan sport coat paired with matching slacks atop his muscled legs...

With a backside to match.

Get your mind off *his backside.*

Stop thinking of how those perfect mounds would feel, clenched and naked against your palms, as his thighs slide between yours...

Ohhhhh...*my.*

"Hmmm?" I hope he does not expect more. Likely, he does not. These moments come upon me often. It is a bizarre mix of the awe I felt when we first met and reverent thanks for his simple aliveness—meaning I am now an idiot barely capable of logic or speech.

The sensation is...

wonderful.

And troubling.

I am rarely described by anyone, myself included, as the fanciful one in the room. And while Cassian Court is often labeled as New York's crown prince, I spent much of my adult life just steps away from real royalty. True, the halls of Palais Arcadia, on the Mediterranean island I called home until two months ago, would not qualify as a *wing* of some New

York buildings—but they were perfect training wheels for the world I am now a part of. Many times, even in the center of, as Cassian's...

What?

As I gaze at his chiseled face, the query burns deeper than ever. *What* am *I to him?* Girlfriend? Companion? The ideal decoration for his arm...for now? Or...something else? Something he does not want to see nor even has to, thanks to the giant whale still flopping in the middle of the room between us. A whale possessed by a ghost named Lily Rianna Court.

His wife.

Until four years ago.

It is the sole detail I can get out of anyone about her— including the man's own mother. Yes, I have tried. And *tried*. Struggled to give him time and room to come to me—the considerations I did not give him the night I first learned about Lily. Instead I stormed off, making him chase me across a park—

The park he left on a stretcher. With three bullets in his body.

"Knock knock." Cassian's playful tone wrestles me from the flashback. He taps a finger to my forehead. "Anyone home?"

I gaze at his retreating hand. Despite my dark reminiscence, fresh need curls low in my belly. Finger porn, Cassian Court style, is not a temptation for which I have girded this afternoon. "*Désonnum,*" I mutter, jerking my stare to meet his instead...

As if that helps.

His eyes have turned smoky—and an alluring kind of reproving. When I use native Arcadian, it hits him like an aphrodisiac. I have not simply "guessed" at this fact. He made sure I knew it shortly after the shooting, when he was still horizontal in a hospital bed and unable to do anything about it. Since then, we have certainly been able to do a few things about it—just not all the "things" we did before that terrible night.

Things he always had such perfect names for.

I want to fuck the color from your eyes, Mishella.

Take me deeper, favori.

Of course you can come a fourth time for me, little girl.

We have dealt with the dearth. We have had to. Compensated in ways our relationship definitely needed. We have been on real, honest-to-Creator *dates.* Have seen some movies (he likes Tim Burton and Peter Jackson), flown out on some day trips (I have decorated his refrigerator with tacky tourist magnets from Niagara Falls, the Hudson Valley, and the White House), and even gone bowling and sailing (a thousand gutter balls and a sunburn of my own later, I am in love with both). I have learned about his love for omelets and bacon and good Scotch. He has learned I prefer milk chocolate over dark—and now, thanks to him, cannot get enough of New York street tacos and red velvet cupcakes from Billy's Bakery.

By all the rules of a "good" relationship, we have done very well.

Good.

It is a category. A definition.

For a relationship that has none.

Moments like this are simply the silent, screaming proof of it. Where even désonnum does not belong. As our stares weave tighter and tighter, a tapestry unfurls, brighter and brighter—and I suddenly see every thread of his thoughts and every color of his soul as if they are my own.

We smile.

He lowers his hand. Scoops mine into it.

"The director was just saying that much of the stained glass in the museum wasn't acquired until the nineteen seventies," Cassian explains. "But that now, it's a crucial part of the Cloisters' collections."

"Oh." I blink, focusing on the large glass pieces. "Hmm. Very interesting." Lying on top of lusting now—in the glow from large glass panels where every figure has wings, a halo, or both.

Yes. Hell-bound.

The man to whom Cassian is referring, a handsome fellow with the beginnings of gray around his angular face, warms and then preens. The "Cassian Court Effect" has claimed another victim. I have yet to meet anyone in this city, from car valets to waitresses to heads of huge corporations, who is immune to it—the largest casualty, of course, being the girl in the mirror. It is a sentence I fully accept—though at first, it was like turning my skin inside out. After twenty-three years of learning to see only the scheming side of humanity, it has been strange—and amazing—to shift my lens, seeing things through Cassian's focus. He stuns me, this man with the shadows in his eyes and the ghosts from his past, who can still rouse so much of the light in others. Or perhaps that is the drive behind his laser focus on it—that seeing the Eden in others helps banish the hell in him.

In that case, maybe I am glad that is my destination too.

"What an honor and privilege it has been to escort you through the museum this afternoon, Mr. Court." The director still glows as we make our way out of the little stone room, into a pair of galleries lined with elaborate medieval tapestries. "Rarely do we get a chance to see our benefactors outside of the fundraising special events, which are usually such clusterf—"

As the man colors, Cassian smirks. "It's all right, Blythe. You're among friends." He wraps an arm around my waist. "Fly that clusterfuck flag with pride."

The man chuckles—and clearly enrolls himself as a new member of the Cassian Court Fan Club. As its president, I join him in worshiping the man with my upturned smile—though the next moment, it is impossible to even remember Blythe's presence. As soon as Cassian dips his head to return my gaze, electricity arcs and zaps and binds us, even stronger than before...heat rocketing into desire, and then desire coiling into lust, as the world spins far away and we breathe hard together, barely recalling we are in public and cannot simply shred each other's clothes away...

"Shall we continue out to the garden?"

Cassian blinks. His jaw compresses before his head jerks up, a forced smile on his strong, sensual lips. Hell overtakes me prematurely, simply having to stare at those lips instead of pulling them to mine...and then to other places...

"Of course," he tells Blythe, shooting me an apologetic glance while slipping his grip from my waist to my hand. It is certain and commanding, his thumb caressing my knuckles as we follow the director out to the little square courtyard, with its lush plants, manicured lawns, and stone fountain surrounded on all four sides by arched walkways. The echo of our steps on the stones seems a perfect—and agonizing—echo of the desire pinging through our bodies.

By all the powers.

When we make it through the garden and finally enter another soaring chapel, I press back into Cassian's side. Perhaps letting his arm rub my chest will relieve at least the ache in my breasts...

And the pillars will magically turn into soaring red velvet cupcakes.

"The Romanesque Hall and the Langon Chapel," Blythe rambles on.

I smile and nod in all the right places, attempting to focus on his litany.

Constructed in stone sourced from Moutiers-Saint-Jean...
Burgundy, France...
in the grand gothic architectural style...

"Gothic." Cassian is more engaging than I can hope to be, even adding one of the most classic versions of his subtle smile. "Well, obviously."

"Oh, *oui*!" The director laughs loudly, earning himself high-holy glares from a cluster of women nearby. Cassian fields it like the verbal version of a fist bump, encouragement and camaraderie in a pleasant mix. I am as grateful for it as Blythe, because I now start to wonder if the man is actually making a play for Cassian. That should make me amused, but...does not. The sensation getting in its way is a complete flummox. What is this twisting in my belly, this irksome stab in my chest?

The feeling intensifies as the director claps a hand to Cassian's shoulder and starts regaling us with details of the chapel's ceiling. I am not as easily "called" as Cassian, barely listening to the narration, even as Blythe guides us to a small side doorway, through a portal accessed by a swipe of his museum key card, and then up a flight of private stone steps into private offices and event preparation rooms. As the men continue to talk, I am only interested in the man's rapt stare at Cassian—even as he swings another door wide and shows us onto a balcony with a jaw-dropping view of the sunset over the Hudson.

That is only where the magic begins.

The alcove is aglow, though not by artificial means. A hundred white candles burn in ornate medieval candelabra, their stone bases carved with a menagerie of animals and—of course—angels. More candles are arranged in the center of a table set for two, with a plate of fresh meats, cheeses, and vegetables accompanied by a tall bottle of Italian red wine. Another plate holds an assortment of fancy desserts. The air is a rich mix of sinful and spiritual, the savory food blending deliciously with the tapers' warm wax.

"*Oh*." I gasp it before I can help it. While the museum tour has been wonderful despite Blythe's bizarre behavior, this is the last—but absolutely best—thing I have fathomed as a grand finale. A medieval-style dream come to life, with my own gorgeous knight.

I *hope* that is what the *two* chairs mean...

Especially when Blythe lifts both brows expectantly at Cassian and then prompts, "Wellll?"

Cassian squares his shoulders. Sweeps an appraising look across the balcony. As a result, *I* do not stop gazing at *him*. Is he adopting "CEO Face" just for me? He knows what it does to me; I have *told* him in words of his own language—words borrowed from my best friend Vylet, a self-proclaimed "Americano junkie," to make sure he understands the point, loud and clear.

Turn-on. Panty dissolver. Invitation to lick.

Without looking at me—another purposeful move?—he pivots his attention back toward Blythe. Waits through one more pause before speaking.

"It's perfect." He grins big, hauling the other man in for a one-shouldered bump. "Thank you, Blythe. Can't express my gratitude enough."

"Oh, you already *do*, Mr. Court." Before I can decipher *that* bit of gushing, the man is back in professional mode, bowing to both of us with formality rivaling any Sancti Palais page from back home. "With that, I bid a fond *bon soir.* Simply pick up the red courtesy phone when you're ready to depart. Security will phone your car to the front and let you out."

"Outstanding."

Blythe bows low over my hand before leaving completely, ensuring I stand in a pool of my own confusion as soon as he shuts the door and is gone. Though I direct my frown out toward the glistening waves and watercolor-bright sky, my unease has not escaped Cassian's observance. Not that I expected it to. The man has been my personal mind reader since the moment we met.

"All right." He demands it in a murmur against my hair, tucking me close to his body. "Out with it."

"With what?"

"You *really* giving me that, *armeau*?"

"And are you really using *that* word...now?"

Armeau. It is not a term he throws around lightly— because he knows that I do not. The Arcadian word for "gift" carries a double meaning, used to denote a person who is special above others in a person's life. When used, it...*elevates* a conversation.

"Sure as hell am." Though his reply comes without a skipped beat, he lets one pass while drawing up and relocking our stares. "You're troubled. Why?"

I wrestle my gaze away. Turn it back to the horizon, banking that the sunset will hold it still for more than a few seconds. The gamble was worth it. The sky is a palette of pink and orange, the river a collection of purple and gold. I walk to the balcony's edge. For a moment, I can truly imagine we are a knight errant and his lady, enjoying a respite as day transforms into night. "There is no room for troubled here." I hope my peaceful breath proves how much I mean it.

"You accuse me of pulling the armeau card, then use a line like that?"

Dismissive shrug. "Worth a try."

Cassian chuckles hard enough to make me join in. Soothes my frayed nerves a little more by stepping behind me, caging me against the stone ledge, hands flattened just next to my elbows. "You weren't comfortable during the tour."

I shift a little. Enough to assure myself his warmth is real...

Including the stiff ridge between his thighs.

"Not true." I curl one of his arms forward, around my waist. *More*... I want so much more. Though keeping our hands from each other would be a feat close to achieving world peace, his recovery from the shooting has stopped us short from being fully passionate for the last six weeks—meaning everything about his nearness coats my senses like a wizard's spell. His scent, cedar and soap and musk. His muscles, now leaner but more defined because of the changes in his workouts. His masculine force, potent and stringent, as if trying to gash its way out of his body and into mine. "The tour, I was very comfortable with."

"But...?"

His voice vibrates along my ear. I swallow, struggling not to let that fire course through the rest of me...but as my toes burn with it, I embrace the defeat. "But Blythe..."

"Blythe?" He jerks back. Just a little. "You're in a twist about *him*?"

"He..." My lips purse. Borrowing serenity from the sky,

despite how the man swirls heat through my belly with tiny circles of his fingers, I push on. "He...wants you, Cassian. In *that* way."

He resettles behind me. Expands the caresses, playing at the top of my panties through my light cotton dress, while teasing my neck with a soft chuckle. "Is that all?"

I take my turn for a little jerk. "Is that *all*?"

"I've known the man for years, Ella. And he isn't subtle."

"Isn't—? Wait. You mean he's...tried to..."

"*Tried.*" He has the nerve to chuckle about it. "Long ago."

"*How* long?"

"Long enough."

"And...and did you...errrm...*return* his...his..."

Another chuckle, huskier and sexier, before he dips in to nip at the space beneath my ear. "What do *you* think?"

I squirm. Battle through the steam he has thickened through my senses with his oh-so-talented fingers and lips. "I think you are a man of many passions—"

"*Specific* passions." He trails that incredible mouth down, lining my shoulder with tingles of perfect heat. "Most particularly, for strawberry blondes with the sky in their eyes and heaven in their kiss." One of his hands sprawls across the front of my throat, compelling me tighter against him. "Oh yeah...and accents. Ones that remind me of Mediterranean islands with trellises full of possibilities..."

Even in my confusion, I smile. His reference to the night of our first kiss, when he scaled a trellis to get onto my balcony and then into my bedroom, can bring nothing else. "But only one of us in that room was still a virgin, Cassian. And I can accept that, even if I do not understand all of it—"

"And I don't want you to." His voice, deepening with

new solemnity, sends vibrations of emotion through me. And confusion.

"But—"

"Ssshhh."

"*Cassian*. We have been open with each other since the start..." When we had to negotiate the terms of the contract that brought me here. Forty million of his dollars. Six months of my life. And the possibility of having exactly this. A connection my spirit has never felt with anyone...

"And I'm being open with you now." He turns me back to face him, stroking tendrils of hair from my face as the wind kicks up—and pointedly clearing his throat as our lower bodies fit against each other again. "As a matter of fact"—his brows jump and his nostrils flare—"if I'm any *more* open about things..."

Against my better instinct, my lips tip up. Against the same intuition, let him see the shudder claiming me as we mesh, soft to hard, woman to man...*perfection*. "I...I do not want you to think I am prying. It is not my place. In just four months—"

He does not allow me to finish. Correction: commands me not to, in the form of a kiss bordering on punishing. His mouth is so incessant, half the air punches from my lungs. The other half funnels strength into my arms, seizing him by both biceps as our lips crush and meld and ravish each other.

A cacophony of heat and heartbeats later, he draws back, gaze thick with sage smoke. "I've imposed few rules about this whole thing, favori," he utters. "But right now, I'm invoking a new one." His hand moves in, spreading across the back of my head. "No more countdowns." His fingertips curl in, pulling at my hair. "I need to have this." Tightens even harder. "Just this. Just...you. Okay?"

He yanks a third time. I let my head tilt, succumbing to the bite of pain. Slide my eyes closed for an instant. "Okay."

His grip eases a little. "So we're good?"

"Good." I manage to volume into it. "Yes. Of—of course. We are good." *Just do not stop holding me like this.* "We are completely...squalid."

He chuffs. "You mean *solid*?"

"Oh. Hmm. That makes sense."

He brushes his lips down over mine again. Raises back up enough to murmur, "You sure about that?"

"About what?"

"Me. Making sense." He dips both hands back down—pulling me harder against him, making my legs widen for him. "Maybe I need to *show* you solid, instead of just telling you."

"*Ahhh.*" It spurts out on a gasp as my limbs shudder, my skin tingles, and my sex pulses. My head falls back again, whirling in a new vortex of color and feeling, letting Cassian completely take over again. I am lost in his ruthless strength as he lifts me to the balcony's thick brick ledge. Engulfed in blood red, in the sunset that bathes his taut, sharp face. A delighted quarry of joy, without sorrow or penance. If we *are* in hell, I gladly relinquish my rights to heaven.

This story continues in Pretty Perfect Toy Temptation Court Book Two!

ALSO BY ANGEL PAYNE

Temptation Court:
Naughty Little Gift
Pretty Perfect Toy
Bold Beautiful Love

Cimarron Series:
Into His Dark
Into His Command
Into Her Fantasies

Suited for Sin:
Sing
Sigh
Submit

The Bolt Saga:
Bolt
Ignite
Pulse
Fuse
Surge
Light

Honor Bound:
Saved
Cuffed
Seduced
Wild
Wet
Hot
Masked
Mastered
Conquered
Ruled

Secrets of Stone Series:
No Prince Charming
No More Masquerade
No Perfect Princess
No Magic Moment
No Lucky Number
No Simple Sacrifice
No Broken Bond
No White Knight
No Longer Lost
No Curtian Call

Lords of Sin:
A Fire In Heaven
Promise of Your Touch
Redemption
Surrender of the Dawn
Tradewinds

**For a full list of Angel's other titles,
visit her at AngelPayne.com**

ABOUT ANGEL PAYNE

USA Today bestselling romance author Angel Payne loves to focus on high-heat romance starring memorable alpha men and the women who love them. She has numerous book series to her credit, including the action-packed Bolt Saga and Honor Bound series, Secrets of Stone series (with Victoria Blue), the intertwined Cimarron and Temptation Court series, the Suited for Sin series, and the Lords of Sin historicals, as well as several standalone titles.

Angel is a native Southern Californian, leading to her love of being in the outdoors, where she often reads and writes. She still lives in Southern California with her soul-mate husband and beautiful daughter, to whom she is a proud cosplay/ culture con mom. Her passions also include whisky tasting, shoe shopping, and travel.

Visit her at AngelPayne.com